25^{95}

NEW

REEFER
MOON

Published by
Evening Post Publishing Company
Charleston, South Carolina
with Joggling Board Press

Editors: John M. Burbage/Susan Kammeraad-Campbell
Designer: Gill Guerry

First printing 2009
Printed in the United States of America

A CIP catalog record for this book has been applied
for from the Library of Congress.

ISBN: 978-0-98-187358-9

Acknowledgements

Sincere thanks
to John M. Burbage,
Susan Kammeraad-Campbell
and Pierre Manigault, my special
"reefer moonies," who believed
in this book when New York
publishing houses
did not.

REEFER MOON

Roger Pinckney

Evening Post Publishing Co.
Charleston, South Carolina

with Joggling Board Press

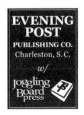

For Jasmine

 **ONE**

The King Air came out of the west whining low over marsh flats and cedar hummocks, climbed into an indigo sky above the Atlantic, banked and circled the deep-green woods. The beach shone like new copper ribbon against an ocean of hammered steel.

A pilot and two passengers. The pilot was good enough to get them there and back provided the weather didn't turn too nasty too fast and his nose was not too deep into cocaine. He had snorted a line earlier with coffee but left his stash in the car.

A tropical storm, the first of the season, had stalled the night before off Vero Beach far to the south, leaving clear skies from Atlanta to Daufuskie Island and only a twelve-knot headwind. Two hours to the South Carolina coast, an hour and three quarters back. Nothing to pick up; nothing to drop off. Easy money if the check cleared. And what was folded in his back pocket – a thousand dollar check with Daufuskie Island Investments embossed in red and blue – looked good or the pilot would not have fired the engines.

It was signed by Poogey Drake, a big man who sweated profusely, especially under his arms, even at 2,500 feet. He had squeezed himself in to the leather back seat. He wore a light-blue oxford-cloth shirt, khaki pants and an alligator belt with a monogrammed gold buckle. His eyes bulged when he was excited, which he was at the moment.

The other passenger, who had climbed into the cockpit as if he were the co-pilot, was tanned, trim and gray with a gold chain hanging loosely around his neck. He left the top two buttons of his red-and-white seersucker shirt open so you could see the chain, and his sleeves turned up to show off a wristwatch as big as a biscuit with diamond chips set into the bezel. Poogey Drake called him Sam.

As the plane approached the island, Poogey leaned forward, clasped Sam's shoulder and shouted, "Daufuskie, Sam! She's as pretty as I said." Daufuskie Island, South Carolina – the name means "sharp like a feather" in Muskegan, but the natives were long gone.

At the sound of the plane, a flock of snowy egrets rose from the shallows of a tidal pond and wheeled like wind-blown paper.

"You can't eat scenery," Sam said. "What you want from me?"

"Land."

"How much."

"Four hundred acres."

"Wouldn't know an acre if I saw one," Sam said. "Talk money."

Poogey Drake sat silent for a minute, and a minute covers a lot of ground at 125 knots, as the pilot headed east until he ran out of island, then swung south over the beach just above the breakers. Sam kept his eyes on the sea as the plane circled again.

Below was a cluster of seaside cottages – swatches of pastel blues, pinks and greens amidst a wide strip of dune scrub highlighted by glints of metal roofs in the afternoon sun. Just inland was a golf course with only nine links winding through trees and near a scattering of structures – an inn, a clubhouse, a golf cart shed, a tennis court and the turquoise sheen of a swimming pool. Even from five hundred feet, they could see leaves in the water and grass in cracks of the concrete.

"One million to build the back nine," Poogey said.

Sam snorted. "Hell, man, you can't even make the front nine pay!"

Poogey's eyes bulged some more, looking like old-time shooter marbles about to explode from his red fist of a face. "Nine, eighteen or even twenty-seven, you don't make money on golf. It's just a game. You make money off real estate, Sam."

"I assume you're talking about an unsecured debt?"

"Can't have the land encumbered. We get a clear title, then borrow on it to build the back nine. Waterfront's good, Sam, but there's only so much of it. Nothing makes value as fast as a fairway."

Sam rolled his eyes, sighed loud enough for the pilot to hear him. "OK. Show me," he said.

Poogey touched the pilot's elbow and pointed to a patch of tall pines toward the middle of the island. On the other side of the trees were two fields with row after row of what looked like little green hives. In a third field sat a dull blue tractor, and a man standing beside it looked up as the King Air banked.

"What's that?" Sam asked.

"Tomatoes," Poogey said. "I'm trying to sell lots and that poor bastard down there is growing tomatoes. Tomatoes! He has to ferry over his plants, ferry his fertilizer, ferry his herbicides and his cigarettes and his beer and his fuel and his migrant crew, come picking time. And when he's done, he has to ferry his tomatoes and everything else back to the mainland. Then he has to put the tomatoes in a truck and haul 'em to Savannah. There are tomato fields all over that anybody can get to with a truck and that guy grows 'em on an island without a bridge ... Tomatoes, my ass!"

"You know a lot about him," Sam said.

"We'll do him a favor when we buy him out."

"Will he see it that way?"

"Probably not, but he doesn't actually own those fields. His father does."

"Who's his father?"

"The Honorable Clarence H. Yarboro, retired. Shot a couple of men a while back for who knows what and had to leave the bench."

"Dead?"

"Yep, one got it square between the eyes and the other just above the left ear as he turned to run."

"Not a judge you want to piss off."

"I guess not."

"You talk to him?"

"Yep, even took him a jug of brown liquor."

"What's he like?"

"Drunk."

Poogey Drake tapped the pilot's elbow again and pointed back toward the last of the pastel-colored cottages. "Buzz it."

The pilot grinned, happy to get something resembling a rush on a dull summer afternoon. He tickled the throttle, dropped the nose, and the engines went from a steady whine to a sudden scream.

A slim, blonde woman ran out of the house on the third pass. She wore a white summer dress down to her ankles and it fluttered in the ocean wind. She was tall and raised her hands to shade her face as she looked up at the plane. Her eyes flashed as blue and as bright as beer-sign neon. Her dress clung to her slightly rounded belly, trim hips and perfectly pointed breasts.

"That's my wife, Susan," Poogey said. "I gave her that house on Mother's Day not long after she turned thirty. Spends her summers down there."

Sam raised an eyebrow. "All summer? By herself?"

"Plenty in Atlanta to keep me busy, and we got no kids."

Sam grinned, then turned serious again. "You know what bothers me about this place? That tomato farmer down there has to ferry all his stuff. You will too."

"For us, the ferry's a plus, Sam. You read the papers. People are scared of each other. You got Jigs killing Jigs over cocaine ..."

The word made the pilot's nose itch.

"... and you got Mexicans sticking up filling stations. You got Rednecks all drunk up and fighting over fat girls in beer joints. You got A-rabs blowing up Jews and vice versa. Anywhere you go anymore, somebody wearing a badge and a name tag wants to x-ray your shoes."

The plane cut back over the salt marsh. "You know anybody who got robbed?" Sam asked.

"I don't and you don't either but that doesn't matter. It's what people think, Sam. Atlanta's clearing forty acres of trees a day – a day! – to make way for vinyl villages with chain link fences and bubbas with pistols manning the gates."

Poogey pointed to the river, coming up fast and wide as the aircraft skirted the island's north shore before turning again.

"We got twenty million people in the big city, half a day away. We got hundreds of thousands more in Charlotte and Raleigh. Everybody's headed south for a piece of paradise. And here's three miles of beach, five thousand acres of woods surrounded by deep water, the best security system in the world. You can leave your door unlocked for a month down there because nobody won't steal nothin'."

"So, for us the ferry's a plus ..." Sam mused. "You already writing ad copy?"

"Yeah, and so far I got deer standing in the road – and I'm calling it a 'Daufuskie Traffic Jam!' And picture a guy in a beach chair with a fishing rig and a caption saying, 'High Crime Area, Something Stole His Bait.'"

Poogey paused, salivating over his words, pursing his fat lips, almost slobbering on himself. "The money will grow like kudzu. All we need is some federally insured magic rain."

Sam sighed again. "You also got a judge who blew two men's brains out under questionable circumstances; and you want to float a loan and maybe skim construction money and kite some lots, and you say there's no crime down there? Great God, man!"

"No *serious* crime," Poogey said. "None that would make the news-papers."

"What about your judge?"

"Like I said, I took him a bottle."

"I know, but did he make the newspapers?"

"Yeah, some, but it died down. Besides, that was across the river."

The pilot turned the aircraft northwest back toward Atlanta, and the sea haze gave way to rippled heat off dry red clay and then to city smog. He radioed the tower and was cleared to land at Hartsfield.

Poogey Drake and Sam soon crawled into the back of a waiting black Lincoln Continental, which sped away. The pilot returned to his third-floor condo just off Peachtree, to the United stewardess he'd been banging; back to waiting for the next call and to staring at his loan-payment books and to feeding the nasty habit gnawing at his brain, corroding the cartilage in his nose. He soon forgot about the flight and his passengers. To him it was just another real estate deal from the air – little men, big plans.

 # TWO

Yancey Yarboro was in his tomato field when his tractor broke down, again, and the plane flew over, swung low and circled overhead. Yancey fiddled with the tractor's carburetor. The float hung up; the engine lurched and smoked. As usual, he had jumped off the tractor and banged the hood with the back of his skinning knife, and stomped and cussed and tinkered and sweated and tried to restart the engine so he could resume harrowing or planting or spreading fertilizer or cultivating or bush-hogging or whatever he had to do that day. But the engine would not restart this time. A flood of gasoline steamed down the side of the block and Yancey shut it down so it would not light up like napalm. He'd seen napalm light up before; he did not want to see it again. He had been to war, came back home, alive, and was farming tomatoes on his daddy's ground.

Yancey Yarboro looked like Nathan Bedford Forrest, the old Confederate general who never lost a cavalry fight – the same general whose men broke down and cried when he told them they couldn't kill Yankees anymore. The lines etched around Yancey's nose gave him a fish-hawk scowl. His eyes reflected an obscure measure of what some might consider kindness. He was as trim as an oak board and moved like he was twenty, but time and war, sun and wind, cigarettes and booze made him look as old as he was, maybe older.

And now he stood there looking over his tractor and then up as the plane passed over. He pawed through the toolbox, grabbed a screwdriver and some wrenches and wondered if he really wanted to fix it or go have a beer and a toke and come back in the cool of the evening if the bugs weren't bad. The plane droned like a skeeter. He wanted to reach up and swat it.

They'll land on the beach, he thought. They did that from time to time. They'd put down and tramp through the dunes and into the woods. The real estate man would spin up visions of a cute cottage with a white picket fence, of sunsets and moonrises, of children building sand castles and a clothesline with beach towels flapping in the wind.

The real estate man would omit important details – like the bugs, copperheads, rattlers and cottonmouths, and the gators, sharks, stingrays and jellyfish, and the mandatory hurricane evacuations when the sheriff showed up at your door and gave you ten minutes to pack one bag and leash the dog. He'd cuff you if you would not go. And the power that flickered every time a frog farted, and the phones that always died when it rained.

He would not mention the aggravation of living in a place you could not get to by car, the endless complications, the carpenters who missed the boat, the tools they forgot, the materials that did not arrive on time. And once you got your house built six months behind schedule and a hundred thousand dollars over budget, the things you forgot to buy when you took the ferry over to go shopping, and how life is without light bulbs and toilet paper. And how your wife takes the scenery for granted and misses the yoga and the yogurt.

The clients would walk around and listen to what the real estate man chose to tell them, and they'd get ticks and chiggers they would not find until after they got home. Land would change hands once in a while for more money than Yancey could comprehend, but there had been no houses built on the island in five years and that suited him fine.

He saw them coming, island by island, slowly at first, then faster like a plague. The strip malls with only a couple of trees left standing for looks, the condos that the swindling sons of bitches called "villas." The gates with guards in bwana helmets and the housing tracts misnamed "plantations" and the golf courses, green and serpentine and strangely beautiful slithering through the woods. The eagles were gone now and the ospreys were few, and gators had moved into the water hazards.

Yes, they had tried it on Yancey's island – spent one hundred million dollars trying – only there was no bridge. Their Gucci shoes could not save them and they drowned, like Pharaoh's host in the old slave spiritual, going down, down in a sea of red ink, the swindling sons of bitches.

The moon was three days short of full and Yancey's head bothered him again thanks to a bit of Chinese copper that the surgeons dared not remove. The slug had wanged off the hood of the armored vehicle, burst through the windshield and into his mouth, and that slowed it enough not to kill him. Now he has one government tooth that does not match and a sliver of metal embedded in his brain, and the moon was working on him like it always did.

Sometimes it sounded like a dentist's drill, sometimes like the whistle of a freight train through the pines at midnight setting the owls to hooting – a steam whistle like you don't hear anymore. Sometimes the noise was like the squeal and squall when you fiddle with the dial of a shortwave radio and can't quite get a signal. It always came with the waxing moon and made him do fool things sometimes.

Fool things like hunting wild hogs in the salt marsh. Fool things like running them with hounds and diving into the squealing melee and killing one with a knife because it was too close to shoot between the dogs. Fool things like wading into the surf and casting bait among a school of black-tip sharks feeding so shallow their bellies rubbed the bottom while their backs shone in the afternoon sun. Fool things like blowing three hundred dollars in a Savannah strip joint and bringing Tara Lynn home at closing time.

She was a strawberry blonde with quick green eyes, and when she danced she jiggled in all the right places. Just thinking about Tara Lynn made Yancey feel like he'd eaten ice cream too fast. After her show, she put on her street clothes – a little fishnet blouse and jeans that fit like a second skin and fringed, high-heeled drum majorette boots – and turned that marvelous rump toward him and shifted from one foot to the other so he could see her muscles ripple through the denim. She grabbed a pool cue, laid four quarters on the table, racked the balls, smiled like a sunning gator and asked, "Winner take all?"

He broke and scratched. She knocked off three balls straight. Yancey sank four, then missed on purpose to see what would happen next. She nicked the eight with the fourteen and the black ball disappeared into a side pocket and they hung up their sticks and, hand in hand, were out the door.

Yancey led her to his pickup, drove to the foot of the Thunderbolt bridge and parked among the rusty trucks and cars of the night fishermen. They walked down the causeway to his skiff, which he had pulled up beneath the bridge, and they sped over to Daufuskie in the dark to his little house on the back side of the island. He fired the hurricane lamps because the power was off again and threw her onto the rumpled sheets and took her with a rush as their shadows danced upon the wall.

She liked him well enough to stay all the next day. They slept late and she fixed him breakfast, the first woman to do so in years. They drank Red Stripe all afternoon and made love again at sunset. She unhooked his belt with her teeth, lifted his shirt and rode him to oblivion.

He took her back to Savannah and through bloodshot eyes watched her dance again. When a fat man, his arms covered in tattoos, reached up like he was going to slip a twenty into her g-string, then grabbed instead, Yancey clipped him in the head with a beer bottle, which shattered and laid him out cold. The man's buddies didn't like it.

Yancey got out of the joint with a split lip, a black eye and sore ribs. Made it to his boat before the cops did. Two weeks later when he came back 'round looking, Tara Lynn was gone.

And now the plane was gone and the moon was coming full again, his head hummed, his tractor was dead and he hadn't had a woman in months. He moved into the shade at the edge of the field and sat down. He felt eyes upon him.

Copperheads will do that sometimes, coil up and stare. When Yancey was a kid, he sat in the dark beneath a tree like this, waiting for daylight and deer to come for acorns. *Tick, tick, tick.* At first he thought it was a foraging mouse. But when the noise did not stop, he turned on his flashlight and saw the copperhead an arm's length away, tickling leaves with the tip of its tail, poised to strike. Yancey hopped backward, landing on his buttocks like a pogo stick and, at that moment, realized why the Negroes call them *oak rattlers*.

But what he saw this time was no snake. It was a battered brogan, the leather cut away to accommodate bunions, calloused brown toes peeking through, a tattered denim cuff and a knobby ankle. "Jesus, Gator Brown, you scared the hell out of me!" Yancey yelled.

"Ain' no harm in dat," Gator Brown said. "Good to be scaid sometime."

Gator Brown was the color of pecans and he gimped along with a myrtle stick carved with mystical signs and painted bright red, orange and mostly blue, a tuft of crow feathers bound just below the handle. Everybody figured him half crazy.

Yancey wrestled his pulse back to something like normal. "What you doing roamin' round in this heat?"

"Weather comin'," Gator Brown said. "Make me all itchy inside."

"You see the plane?"

"Yessir, white folk dey still lookin'. You broke down 'gain?"

"Yeah. I got the carburetor fixed but still won't start."

"Dat a Fode fuh you. Ought 'a get a mule."

"I'll take my Ford," Yancey said. "Mule too slow."

"Mule fassa 'n dat tractor now. Mule eat grass, ain' need no gas."

"It'll run after the engine cools down. I'll come back this evening."

"Wan' a ride?"

"In the wagon?"

"Why sho'," Gator Brown said as he pointed to the edge of the field. "Henrietta ain' mind. She tie up ober dey."

"Henrietta?"

"Dat right, Henrietta Fode."

So off they creaked, Gator Brown holding the reins, talking Henrietta down the sandy lane, Yancey sitting beside him on the weathered board seat. They rolled past shanties with window frames and porch posts painted blue to keep back the evil spirits. Past dirt-swept yards, little gardens full of corn and peas and okra. Past scrabbling chickens, skinny goats and lazy cows tethered out to graze because there were no fences. Past fields grown over in tangles of honeysuckle and briar, magnolias bulging with blossoms big as hubcaps and tall pines whispering sad secrets in the breeze, to a great oak forest with Spanish moss drooping long gray tears from limbs hanging out over the river.

"Weather comin'," Gator Brown said.

THREE

Susan Drake heard the plane, too. She was in the upstairs bathroom with the whirlpool and mirrored walls, working hard at her makeup table dabbing at a fortune in cosmetics.

She was forty, always worried about how she looked. She tanned well but her eyelashes and eyebrows were pale, almost invisible. Her brows nearly met above the bridge of her nose and she did not like that either. So she tortured them with tweezers, plucking hairs, wishing those she left were longer and darker and thicker.

Working a Q-tip, she was cleaning up a tiny smear of mascara at the corner of her eye when the plane made its first pass. *Skeeter plane*, she thought. The county sprayed the island when the bugs were bad and the wind was right. Sounded like the aircraft was coming over the treetops so low and fast that it would suck the blossoms off the oleanders.

But this is good, she thought. She had a date with Chip, Jimmie and Johnny and the bugs would eat them alive otherwise. They would play moonlight golf tonight along with Cassandra, Debbie and Sherida. They'd dress up in negligees, and dress the men, too, petting and fawning over them, making them up like women. They would drink gin and play three holes, and laugh and wiggle and hug and kiss and giggle in the moonlight. And when they were done, they'd strip naked and plunge into the clubhouse pool if no one was around, and usually no one was.

Chip, delicate and beautiful, lisped his way through life, a pebble in the shoe of propriety. If you tied his hands behind his back, or handcuffed him as he preferred, you might figure him French – struck dumb, unable to speak without gestures, able only to smirk and smack and tongue his lips.

Chip managed property for the Daufuskie Island Club and Resort whenever there was any to manage. He drew a fair salary while he frittered away the hours, insulting an underling occasionally to keep things interesting, spending the majority of each day forwarding vaguely obscene stories on the Internet to a long list of friends, most of them gay. He rented out the cottages and made sure there were clean towels and tampons and toilet paper in each. If there were a problem, and there were many, all a guest had to do was call Chip and he would make it right with the wit, grace and charm of a Byzantine courtesan.

Women loved him.

Jimmie and Johnny were from Hilton Head and Chip got them passes on the resort ferry whenever Susan Drake wanted to play full-moon golf. They were in the hotel business on the other side of the river where the hotel business was good. The men were strong and handsome and gay, but so standoffish with each other in public you'd never know it unless they told you. They told Susan Drake.

Susan loved Johnny the most. He was six feet, broad shouldered, olive skinned and sensitive, and when she had him over for the evening he would sleep downstairs but wake her with a fresh cup of Colombian coffee each morning, often served with flowers and champagne. Sometimes he would put these gifts on the night stand and shed his silk pajamas and crawl naked with her under the covers, cupping and fondling her breasts, whispering adorations in her ear.

Susan was married, but she told herself it was OK since he was gay.

"God, if you were only straight," she would whisper back.

But he was not. Sometimes Jimmie would get lonesome and come over and get naked too and slip in on the other side of her, and all three would drift off dreaming while the sun rose from the ocean and the surf rolled onto the beach just outside the window. Chip would come upstairs and bounce on the end of the bed and call Susan a slut and a whore. And he'd call Jimmie and Johnny sluts and whores as well.

They would get up around noon, mix up Bloody Marys and sit in the hot tub together for two hours, and then walk on the beach holding hands and picking up shells until it was time for the evening ferry to return to Hilton Head.

That's how Susan spent summers on Daufuskie Island. She sometimes played daylight golf – fully clothed – and enjoyed dinners with neighbors at the beach club, community fish fries and shrimp boils and lots of liquor always. Now Chip and Jimmie and Johnny were coming to play full-moon golf again and she was priming her expectations when the aircraft made its second pass, which the skeeter plane never did.

She was down the stairs and out the front door on the third pass, running through loose beach sand east of the house when the plane came in fast and low over the treetops. She shaded her eyes, looked up and squinted.

The plane banked and she saw a hand at a rear window and she knew it was Poogey. She watched the plane circle and hoped it would land on the beach. When it left and did not return, she walked back to the porch, rinsed the sand from her feet and returned to her chair at the dressing table.

Poogey was not a bad man. He was bull-headed, but he gave much and asked little. They married at nineteen, the prettiest girl in the trailer court and the richest boy in town, so everybody said.

It was almost true. Her father sold hardware to neighborhood stores before Home Depot came through and ruined the trade. So he turned to religion, the snake-handling kind, and spent almost every Saturday rousting copperheads from the boulder fields at the foot of Stone Mountain, just below the great Confederate monument etched in granite there. One evening he brought home a prize diamondback, six feet long and buzzing angrily inside an old orange crate. "Stay away from that box," he warned. "He ain't been to church yet."

But when her father hauled her and the diamondback into church the next morning, Susan got queasy, ran outside and vomited. He took a switch to her for that. He did the same thing when she rode in the back of the bus with a black playmate. Punished for keeping company with black children; punished for not keeping company with snakes. The messages were as twisted as a bucket full of guts.

Susan walked to school and wore her big sister's dresses and was waiting tables at the Dixie Diner when Poogey came in the door and ordered the fried pork chop, two eggs over easy, grits, white toast with butter already on it and a Coke.

He offered to buy her a silver RV Airstream with two bedrooms and a hot tub but she said no. She wanted a Bentley instead. He gave her a Mercedes station wagon and she loved him dearly.

But she miscarried once and when she was pregnant and bleeding the second time and it would not stop, the doctors cut her open. But it all was for naught. What survived the effort was a small scar that would not tan, and like her eyebrows, it worried her always. It was the deep wound that never healed – the one Poogey inflicted on her, although he never realized it.

Daufuskie Island Club and Resort, bankrupt the first of several times, sold Poogey Drake eighteen lots for a half-million dollars. An unfinished house was on one of them. Poogey stumbled through it on a bleary Sunday afternoon in May, brought Susan over later and asked if she liked it. She said she did and he said, "It's yours. Happy Mother's Day." She wept.

Poogey sold a dozen lots and got his money back, and soon after he closed on the other six, he paid to finish the house. She had it painted in pastels and hung on a wall the four-hundred-pound blue marlin she caught off Cabo San Lucas the year before, along with the sailfish from Costa Rica, and the mahi, wahoo and barracuda from the Gulf Stream off Daufuskie. The house had three bedrooms and three baths and a rope hammock on the front porch and soft beach towels and fluffy pillows everywhere.

She came each year the Saturday before Mother's Day and did not go back to Atlanta until Thanksgiving.

Poogey Drake had more time and money than he needed. One January night in Atlanta after he came home with the stench of scotch on his breath and that of another woman everywhere else, Susan grabbed the pistol from the bedside table and fired a bullet just inches above his head and through the wall.

The police did not come and it did not make the newspaper. But it sent Poogey off for treatment. His psychiatrists said he suffered from a complicated addiction to alcohol, cocaine and sex. He came home thirty days later, having sworn off liquor and dope and women forever. That's what he said.

So now she had spent six months on Daufuskie Island for each of the last nine years. She loved her husband and he loved her. But he had his life and she had hers and they got together for the holiday parties with various power brokers – a mayor, some senators and a congressman or two, and occasionally a presidential hopeful.

Poogey Drake was a Republican who raised lots of money for the GOP during election season and drove around with enough bumper stickers to patch the leaks on every roof in shanty town. Susan raised money for hospitals and the arts. She once flew a load of medical supplies to some obscure civil war somewhere that everybody forgot about once it was over.

She also took up hobbies. Two years back she bought an old Pentax camera with all the lenses and roamed around the island taking pictures, mostly black and white. Artsy stuff, close-ups of seashells, the rugged grain of driftwood, the mysterious textures little waves left at low-tide on the beach. Snap, snap, snap, frame after frame, roll after roll. She put the exposed film in a shoebox beneath her bed but she never got around to taking them across the river for processing. After a while, she put the camera away.

People were her favorite hobby. If she made them happy, maybe they would love her. Susan needed love. She enjoyed sex, but love, real love, was what she needed. Like the love of a child. *Oh God, not that again,* she thought as the television weatherman hyped an approaching tropical storm. If they sprayed for the bugs and the storm stayed offshore, Chip and Jimmie and Johnny would come for drinks and moonlight golf and this pleased her greatly.

So Susan Drake traced her lids and brows, daubed her cheeks, dawdled over the lines and contours of her face, looking into the mirror as if it were a window. But she could not see very far.

FOUR

It was May and Christy Seabrook was headed home to Beaufort. The Seabrooks had been there since the beginning: Shipmasters and merchants at first, bankers and farmers later. There was a community called Seabrook, an island, too. He was named for St. Christopher, the patron saint of travelers, the man who bore Jesus across troubled waters. Jesus bore Christy, too. Put up with him actually.

There's a country hymn about coming home on the wings of a dove. Christy blew home that summer on the wings of a storm that boiled up out of the Caribbean a month early dumping rain like shingle nails on iron-fisted winds. Traveling north along U.S. Highway 17 through Georgia was like driving through a six-hour car wash.

The rain slackened as Christy passed through the glistening streets of Savannah and resumed as he crossed the great swamp on the South Carolina side of the river. He took blacksnake local roads through Jasper County and across a long two-lane bridge to the timbered headlands haloed by the lights of Beaufort on the bay.

Christy eased through the biggest puddles and around downed limbs. The wind switched directions as he reached Sully's Place on the edge of town. The eye had passed and the storm would blow itself out by daybreak, gasping its last upon the Blue Ridge. Sully's had concrete-block walls, a tin roof and the usual collection of rust-eaten pickups out front – flap-fendered Fords and degraded Dodges mostly. Another sheet of rain rattled through the palmettos as he pulled into the parking lot.

Christy's neck muscles were fiddle strings, his throat a curing barn, his eyes hot ball bearings, but he was happy. A rainy night, trucks in the lot, beer signs in the window. He was home and starting over.

He chose a stool at the end of the bar and kept his back to the wall, a habit he acquired long ago. He caught the barmaid's eye and pointed at the nearest tap. A girl sitting four stools away reached for her smokes, cutting her eyes in his direction. She lit up, took a drag, exhaled at her reflection in the mirror behind the bar. Through ranks of bottles and glasses and the clutter of jars of pickled eggs, pickled sausage and pickled pig's feet lining the bar, he saw her smile. His first draught went down easy.

An hour later, and he sat at her side. She told him her name, which he promptly forgot. But he did remember two things: She was a receptionist for a new real estate firm on Hilton Head and her boyfriend was a shrimper who had gone to check on his boat in the storm.

You work hard and what you do slowly gets the best of you, coiling and twining around your brain like kudzu. Stockbrokers and insurance men think of the odds, car salesmen of the options. A shoeblack ogles your feet and a barber studies your hair. Running dope is like that, too.

Though Christy could not remember the receptionist's name, he recalled a multitude of women like her – luscious secretaries, travel agents, beauticians and fashion models flying in via Freeport on just their birth certificates after shuffling their passports stamped "Bogotá" home through the mail. The blue-eyed corn-silk blondes, with bright smiles and honest faces, muling carefully sealed packets of Colombian cocaine stashed up both ends, bigger loads dissolved in carry-on liters of Bahamian liqueur.

So he ordered two more beers, one for himself and the other for the girl sitting next to him.

She chattered and giggled while Christy wondered about the shimp-boat. Small ones were typically mortgaged to the scuppers and could be bought, but they couldn't get far off shore. Big ones seldom hauled dope. The skipper could follow the catch clean to Venezuela if he had to, and re-rig for scallops, swordfish, sharks and herring along the way.

Christy figured that someday he would charter a freighter – a two-hundred-foot Panamanian rust bucket he'd scuttle when done. She'd cruise off the coast, lay to every hundred miles or so while his men shuttled loads of marijuana ashore at Jacksonville, Savannah, Charleston. By the time the ship got to New Jersey, he'd be rich enough to quit the business before he went to jail. Christy did not want to go to jail so he never spoke of it. A man could *mouth* himself that way. The *mouth* is a self-fulfilling prophesy, *ju-ju* he could bring on just thinking about it. It was African, like a lot of things in the South, like cast nets and cooking collards, playing blues and mojo. Like the singing in Sea Island churches, baptizing on the falling tide so the river carries the sins out to sea.

His fourth beer went down faster than the third. He was considering or another round and trying to get the girl into his truck for a sample of the Old Thigh Opener, a quarter-pound of weed swept from the deck after delivering his last Florida load. South Carolina's motto is, "While I breathe, I hope." Christy knew that better than anybody.

Suddenly the door swooshed and Christy turned and looked the way everybody turns and looks when a barroom door swings open.

In walked a tall, haggard man, dripping in a T-shirt, jeans, an oil-stained yellow slicker and muddy, white-rubber shrimper's boots. Christy knew he just lost a shot at the receptionist but did not mind. There were more women than shrimpboat skippers.

"Jackie," she gushed.

Jackie acknowledged her with a flick of his eyes. Four long steps and he was between them, leaning on the bar, speaking into the mirror behind it and staring at Yancey's reflection.

"I know you," he said, cocking his head and squinting.

Oh shit, Christy thought. Some men will bust you in the jaw for just looking at their girls.

"I know you," Jackie said again. "That oyster roast at Land's End."

Christy peeled back the years, found nothing.

Jackie's eyes danced. "Yeah, you drove down from your daddy's plantation sunburnt all to hell and ready to howl."

Christy finally dredged up Jackie's face from the blur of good times gone. "Yeah," he said, smiling now. "Whatever happened to the red-head?"

"Married her," Jackie said.

The girl took a sip of beer, mouthed another cigarette with pointed disinterest.

"Where you been?"

"Florida," Christy said.

"Yeah? I get down there sometimes. East coast." Jackie motioned for the barmaid. "You shrimping?"

"Broke'ing," Christy said.

"Seafood, vegetables?"

"Whatever," Christy said as the barmaid brought another round.

They agreed to meet the next morning at the docks. The receptionist showed up, too, dressed like a typical Carolina girl off work – low-cut knitted cotton top, jeans cut off real short and frayed nearly to the crotch, the insides of the pockets hanging down against her flesh like the floppy ears of a young coon hound.

Christy looked her up and down. *Give her a broad-brimmed beach hat, about three days of sunburn, a smear of zinc oxide across her nose and cheeks and she could breeze through Customs*, he thought.

But that would be a cocaine run and Christy didn't run cocaine any more. He bought a little every now and then after the money came in, but left running it to others. Blow was nasty business, could get you killed. Coke smugglers pack automatics, and when they dip into their loads, they often get itchy forefingers.

Christy had an Uzi, a neat little number with two clips in a fitted aluminum case, but hadn't fired it. He swapped two kilos of butt-kick weed for it on the Jacksonville docks when he got started. Every smuggler ought to have an Uzi. Christy also had a shotgun – a sawed-off twelve-gauge pump – but hadn't fired it either. Not as stylish as the Uzi but deadly just the same. He kept the pump loaded with double-ought buck behind the seat of his truck.

Christy had no particular love for guns, but he had a keen desire for reefer. *Marijuana didn't cause hangovers, industrial absenteeism, domestic violence or nuclear war. It did not negatively affect the Dow Jones. It gave the world what it needed more of – reflection, creativity and real good sex. It really was, as the braided and wild-eyed Rasta men proclaimed on the Kingston waterfront, "de breath of God, mon."* That's what Christy thought.

Reefer was cheap down where they grew it, cheap as Bahia grass hay. But reefer appreciated a hundred times in a thousand miles – good math for a man who can stand the heat. Now Christy was back home in South Carolina with an additional 400 miles worth of value. He knew the numbers were good and his chances even better. Too hot now in Florida, in more ways than one.

So there he was on a dock with some broke-dick shrimper, a Carolina girl with her ass cheeks hanging out, a shrimpboat swinging at anchor out on the river and the captain's small flat-bottom launch waiting to get them there.

Jackie went down the ladder first, dropped the last five feet into the skiff and held it steady. Christy followed. The wooden steps were cracked and dried from the weather and stained with sea-bird shit. Below the tide line, the ladder's rungs were slick with algae slime.

The girl came down last, her thin ankles brushing Christy's fingers and once, twice, her calves caressed his face. He liked it, obviously.

"Careful, Sondra," Jackie warned.

And Christy remembered her name – Sondra, not Sandra – so he called her Sondra not Sandra and called him Cap'um Jack. Ten hours after they met, he had given them nicknames and they didn't mind. All was according to plan.

 **FIVE**

Mike McElvern swung the tiller and left the Morgan River chop for the swift green flow of Lucy Point Creek. The hull flexed below his feet, the old Evinrude sputtered as the boat dipped and skittered, slewing like a car on a rain-slick highway. The sky was late-summer blue and off to the southeast a line of squalls stacked up over the ocean. Mike felt bad weather in his bones.

He was blessed as Michael, Anthony, Joseph and Patrick, in that order, thanks to a parish priest befuddled by all the names the child's mother offered. He could have been Tony or Joe or Pat, but for some reason Mike stuck.

His ancestors came over in the 1840s when the potato famine starved them out of Ireland. Besides strong drink, Irishmen have a great affinity for the shovel. Irishmen dug the New York City subways and the Erie Canal. In the South Carolina Lowcountry, they toiled in rice fields for forty cents a day. Slaves were too valuable by then for that kind of labor, something nobody talks about on St. Patrick's Day in Savannah, where truckloads of green beer quickly become a sewer full of green piss and girls flash green titties at the WSAV-TV news cameras.

Mike passed over the shovel for oars. His father, dead a dozen years, had the only sports shop in Beaufort. The place looked like a calendar, the kind shotgun shell companies give away. His father had bait, tackle, used guns, ammunition, weepy outboard motors, a blue-tick hound curled at a potbellied stove and weekly poker games.

A noble crowd sat around the table. They were a diminishing remnant of another century, old men who as young men sailed and rowed out to their favorite fishing drops and back. That was before anybody had outboard motors and mobile homes that never moved, before the endless mesh of strip malls, telephone wires and poles. It was before they shot deer off golf courses at night, back when they bayed them with hounds and brought down venison with buckshot from long-barreled side-by-sides.

Mike's earliest memories were of that shop and those men, of the smell of sweet, two-cycle oil, whisky, cigars, chewing tobacco and of constant wisdom delivered with a garnish of sarcasm. Mike endured the teasing and wanted to be just like them. He wanted to fish and hunt, go off to Carolina and get a degree in English and return to the wheelhouse of his own shrimp boat quoting Tennyson and Shakespeare with a Southern accent.

But his father died the middle of his freshman year at USC, and the doctors and the lawyers took the sports shop. Almost got the house too. So instead of a shrimp boat Mike bought a seepy plywood skiff, a hundred and twenty-five crab pots, and an Evinrude fifty-horse motor that ran on borrowed time. No Tennyson, scant Shakespeare. The only lines he remembered were, "Full fathom five, thy father lies, of his bones are coral made." Mike's father was not buried at sea. He was planted in the cedar shade behind St. Peter's by the Sea on Carteret Street.

Mike dropped his first crab trap that morning where Lucy Creek swung toward the St. Helena Island shore. Ten thousand years of running tides had cut a deep hole there, and it always held Atlantic blue crabs. He used a Coburg Dairy milk jug for a float, which soon wore a beard of sea grass and barnacles, with twenty feet of frayed rope and a wire crab pot tied to the bottom end. The contraption was baited with shrimp trawl by-catch, or chicken backs and turkey necks sometimes. Crabs crawled in the trap, not out.

Mike had never used an electric winch to haul in his traps. He used the "Armstrong Method" instead. He throttled back, swung his skiff down tide and idled alongside the plastic float. No wasted moves. A snatch, three quick overhand pulls and he jerked the wire trap out of the creek and over the gunnels. The motor blubbered smoky bubbles into the murky water as he shook a dozen angry crabs into a rusty steel drum rocking at his feet.

After cramming a fistful of bait into the slot in the middle of the trap, he threw it back overboard. A burst of salt foam and a sudden hiss and the float rattled as the line drew tight. An instant later, he shoved the motor in gear, throttled wide open and the boat was back on plane. Good therapy for a man grieving over good times gone. Only a hundred and twenty-four pots to go – six, eight, ten hours, depending on weather and tide.

Meatball Jenkins – the three-hundred-pound ice, gas and scale man at Spanky Lubkin's Seafood – met him at the dock. Meatball was Gullah, a grandson of slaves, great-great-grandson of West Africans. He hallooed down from his perch between the ice shredder and boom winch. "How dey runnin', Mr. Mike?"

Gullahs speak a language all their own – approximations of English words, a Creole strung like beads on West African grammar served up rapid-fire. Poetic, musical. When a Gullah's belly is full of beer and he really gets going, you wish he came with subtitles.

"Picking up. Should be better by next moon." Mike's face – parched by the sun and salt and wind – crinkled when he spoke.

Meatball lowered the cable and Mike hooked it to one of two steel barrels in the bottom of his boat. The winch clicked and whirred and hauled the catch up to the dock. "Dat good 'cause Mr. Spanky jus' got off de phone to Savannah. Price down two cent."

Mike didn't cuss often but he cussed this time. The Evinrude coughed worse than usual, the hull needed caulk and he still owed Spanky Lubkin a hundred bucks for bait. The winch rattled again, the dock creaked as it took the load and the second steel barrel swung onto the scale.

"Dat de way it be," Meatball said as he slid the weights. "Canner, he bullshit broker. Broker, he bullshit buyer. Buyer, he bullshit crabber man. But crabber man don't bullshit no ribbuh…

"Look here," he added, almost as an afterthought, "somebody been 'round axin' fuh you."

Mike's stomach iced, the freeze shot up his spine. He started the motor, eased the boat out into the current and asked, "Who?"

Meatball shook his head. "Don' worry, Mr. Mike. You know I ain' crack ma teeth 'bout where you is."

Mike swung uptide. "What kind'a clothes he wear?"

Meatball rolled his hat back, scratched his head here and there. "Same as you," he hollered back.

No banker, no cop, not dressed like that. Good. But Mike didn't have long to think about it: Christy was waiting for him in dappled oak shade on the hill not far away.

SIX

Mike knew him, but not well. Son of William and Elizabeth Seabrook of Huspah Plantation over toward Yemassee, a troublesome child shipped off to boarding schools in Yankee land. But he came home every summer a little bigger, a little smarter. Then he came home to stay, but after a single summer on the plantation mending fences, killing snakes, bush-hogging weeds and brush along ditch banks, and watching over a herd of sullen Angus cattle, Christy disappeared. Mike had not seen him in years.

"Hello, Michael," Christy said with a boyish grin as if it had been only yesterday or the day before.

"Christy Seabrook," he replied. "How the hell you been?"

Mike swung the fuel tank up over the tailgate, rolled his lunch bag into his slicker and tossed them in through an open window. A flock of peanut-sized horseflies rose from the dash, buzzed and ricocheted off the windshield and headliner.

"Not bad, not bad. Where you staying at, these days?" Christy asked, drawing each word beyond the usual limits of a Southern accent to reconfirm where he was from.

Mike saw Christy's pickup, all up in chrome and mirrors and clearance lights, parked in the shadows. "Nice ride," he said. "I'm living over on Pine Island."

Christy nodded knowingly. "Watching over things?"

Mike nodded, not sure where the conversation was headed, and stepped forward, offering his hand. Christy took it for an instant and – like a dancer who knows all the moves – reversed his grip and locked thumbs with his childhood friend as if they were in California. "The owner lives up north. I stay in the little house, cut the grass and all."

Christy pressed him. "What's the dock like?"

Mike shrugged. "Gangway, tee-head and a float. Why?"

A battered ice truck – groaning and leaking, one headlight gone – rumbled into the yard, rattled down to the riverbank and backed up to the doors of the fish house. There was a babble of Gullah between Meatball and the driver and the swish and grate of ice blocks sliding into the shed.

"How much water at low tide?" Christy asked.

"Not sure. Six, maybe seven feet. Why?"

"Will the deck stand a load?"

"What kind of load?"

Christy gently took Mike by the elbow and turned him toward the river. "Come on, I'll buy you a Coke."

They walked over to the fish house. Meatball grinned and nodded because the white boys had found each other and obviously there was no bad blood.

Mike and Christy got their drinks, went back outside and sat beneath the oaks on the sagging tailgate of Mike's truck. Mike slaked the salt from his throat.

"It's weed," Christy said. "Jamaican weed and lots of it." The words swiftly and effortlessly rolled from his lips like an incantation. "I need a landing, you know, a quiet place out of the way."

Mike knew the stories – the dope buried and forgotten in the dunes, the bales washing up on the beach with the east wind, the shrimpers who left the dock dead broke and tied up again a couple of mortgage payments ahead. But that was ten years ago.

"Nobody hauls dope on shrimp boats any more," Mike said. "The big boys cornered the market."

Christy smiled, stared off at the marsh and said, "To succeed in this business, Michael, you do what they don't expect. But let me worry about that. Your job will be simple. Just give us the all-clear, some kind of a signal. We'll work out the details later. There's money in it for you."

"How much?"

"Ten thousand dollars."

 # SEVEN

Yancey worked on the tractor while the fields dried out. The island dirt was rich, but always thirsty. The soil took seven inches of rain like most ground soaks up a shower. The puddles sat here and there in low spots, round and bright as silver dollars beneath the brightening sky, smaller and fewer the next day and then they were gone. Another week of hot humid weather and his tomatoes would begin to turn.

Yancey Yarboro grew the best tomatoes on earth in the same Sea Island soil that his ancestors had grown the best long-staple cotton the world had ever known. His tomatoes were big and red and sweet, not those pasty pale bastards from Florida. Most growers picked them green and let them ripen in the backs of semis bound for New York or Boston or Philly, and that's what you got, pasty pale bastards with an aftertaste of diesel smoke. Some picked them pink and sent them to Raleigh, Richmond and Chattanooga. Those were a little better. But Yancey picked his two or three days before dead ripe and sent them across the river to Savannah and they were sold in stores and fruit stands along I-95 from Hardeeville north to Florence. A lot of them busted in shipment but the ones that made it were the best tomatoes in the world. When you bit into one you savored the salt and the strangely sweet juice nourished by centuries of sweat, grief and stubborn pride. And you would like it even if you did not already know the taste or the tale.

This was poetry and Yancey loved poetry as much as he loved any-thing, as much as whisky, women and horses, as much as the tide, trees and moonlight, even though the moon set off the buzz in his brain. His love of this land offset a pain more than most men could bear.

He was in the world – like the Good Book says – but oft times not of it, like John the Baptizer, wound up wild, ready to lay an ax to the trunks of trees bearing bad fruit. And, yea, cast them into the fire.

But he was not John. He was Yancey Yarboro, shot up in the war and growing big juicy tomatoes in his daddy's ground. All of that is poetry and there's no profit in poetry. But there was profit in tomatoes if he could just get his tractor fixed and hire some Mexicans to do the picking. He negotiated for Mexicans every year, cut deals with a labor contractor down in Statesboro.

A good Mexican picker was like a major league baseball pitcher: Glorious to behold, spending far more time in the windup than the pitch. A good one would stand there in the blazing heat of summer, mop his brow, scratch his ass, stare at the sun and shift back and forth on his feet. Then he'd bend over and pick a bushel in forty seconds, straighten up and go back to scratching, staring and shifting. He'd get fifty cents a bushel and so would the man who humped the basket to the end of the row and heaved it onto the trailer. The field boss who clipped the chits got as much as the men who did the picking, the humping and hauling. Each made more than Yancey did with tomatoes.

The migrants came though every summer, each crew with three trucks – the field boss's Caddy strapped to the trailer bed of the first, the pickers on the second, a load of mattresses and coolers on the third.

All the trucks bore extraneous lights, extravagant chrome and names in Spanish like *"Virgin Pequena"* and *"Puta Tomato."* Yancey had to peel the Mexicans away from their stuff, get them over in his skiff to the tomato fields, pick and load and get them back to the mainland when done. It was way too much trouble but he did this anyway.

You cannot get a Gullah to pick tomatoes. Black folks worked so hard in slave times that once they were freed they got together down in the swamp, beat on drums and swore upon the bones of their martyred ancestors never to work again. That's what local white folks claimed as they elbowed each other and joked about it.

Yancey knew the truth was like the taste of his tomatoes, a complicated bouquet, never too sweet, never too dry.

The Gullahs arrived in chains from West Africa. A hundred years later, you'd have to put them in chains to get them to return. Along with freedom, some were given plots of ground here and there. Not forty acres and a mule like the Yankees say, but five acres, maybe ten, a *task*, which is all the land that anybody can work in a day without machinery.

There were no mules after "when gun shoot" in Port Royal Sound and the Federals landed. The invaders rounded up the slaves and worked them hard, even drafted some into the Yankee army, mostly for propaganda. After the troops finally left fifteen years later, the Gullahs grew their gardens, fished, shrimped and oystered, and they bought plows and mules. They got to vote because they had land and there were no Ku Klux on the islands to hassle them. They were isolated and they grew strong, and teachers and preachers and a few bishops rose up from among them. They elected a few of their brothers to the United States Congress.

About a century later, the Damn Yankees returned, this time to steal the beach and waterfront lots, to play golf and tennis and sit around in hot tubs. They threw the demographics all out of whack. Property taxes doubled, tripled, quadrupled. And the able-bodied Gullahs moved to Savannah or Charleston or even to New York City for work, and sent money home to those who could not. And they came home Thanksgiving weekends for family reunions. They went to First African Baptist Church and ate fried chicken, red rice and boiled collard greens, and remembered what it was like when they were children running barefoot along the sandy trails.

Then they had to leave again. Couldn't afford to stay. So Yancey hired Mexicans to pick his tomatoes. Gullahs wouldn't do it anyway.

But first, Yancey needed to fix his tractor. He took his skiff over to Savannah and bought the parts. He thought briefly about stopping at the strip joint for a beer and to see if Tara Lynn was back. But the thought of watching her dance and of her ignoring him while some fat greaser pawed her was too much, so he did not.

He returned to the island and his yard, swatted mosquitoes and endured his love-hate relationship with the moon in his head while he pulled down the carburetor and replaced the float, needle valve and seat. The float in a carburetor is like the float in the back of a toilet. It works when it works and if it doesn't, new parts don't matter.

It did not work the first time, so Yancey took it apart again and he could not see a thing wrong with it. He rubbed the parts with the grit in the skin of his thumbs and when he put it back together, it worked. So he backed the tractor to the mower, lined up the three-point hitch and hooked it up, then drove into the fields to cut the tall grass around the outside rows, to keep the snakes away from his Mexicans.

He was halfway through his second pass when he saw stakes and survey flags fluttering in the woods – his daddy's woods, his woods, as he had come to think of them. He stopped the tractor and stared at the stakes as a black rage rose within, a rage that throbbed with his pulse and echoed with the buzz in his brain.

The flags were orange and red, and there were numbers and letters on the stakes. He thought about pulling them up and throwing them in a pile and setting them ablaze. But the surveyors would know he did it, so he ignored the markers for now; he ignored them as best he could. Later, as he drove his tractor by them, he struggled with a powerful urge to stick them up the ass of the first man he saw in a golf shirt and two-toned shoes. He'd come back after dark and move them – a foot here, two feet there, ten feet at another place, and so on. This would result in great confusion, he decided, numbers that made no sense and lines that did not intersect, even on the far side of Uranus, so to speak.

This would be weeks or months later when they thought everything was ready to go. Meanwhile, he would find out all he could, see who was on which side of what line. Shuffling the stakes would fix those swindling sons of bitches. For a while.

Yancey had no stomach for supper that night but did have a great thirst for blood, so he sat on his porch and drank whisky. He drank it while his dinner got cold and the sun went down and the moon came up, pulling the tide high into the tall marsh grass, higher and higher until just the tops of the reeds showed above the water, a dark fuzz in the moonlight like a blush of rust on bright steel. He drank until the whippoorwills began calling from way out amongst the pines. And then he made his move.

He stumbled from the house and climbed onto the tractor and ran without lights down the same sandy tracks he had ridden before in the wagon with Gator Brown and Henrietta Ford.

Yancey did not know much about Henry Ford, except that he had said you could buy any color car from him so long as it was black. He also knew that a Mr. Kingsford had a contract to supply oak boards for the Model A truck beds, but the planks were too long. The scrap became Kingsford charcoal, the best you could buy.

But Yancey did not buy charcoal. He made his own from hurricane-felled hickory. He laid out venison and wild pig, which he killed when the moon was coming full. This time, as it was coming full again, he headed off to rearrange those survey stakes, to lay the ax to the trunks of trees that did not bear good fruit.

This was poetry again, the kind in the Good Book, and the moon hummed in his head. It was easy to be poetic on a night like this, when the world was lit up like day and the tide was way up into the salt marsh. Yancey was drunk, and he damn near fell off the tractor from the glory of it all.

Then he heard birds. At first they sounded like mockingbirds, bickering in the moonlight, then like sandpipers piping and laughing gulls laughing. But laughing gulls laughed only during the day.

Yancey believed in ghosts, just like everybody else who grew up on the island, and as he stumbled through the cassina bushes behind the seventh tee, he saw them: Gossamer figures in the moonlight fluttering along a fairway wider and longer than they build anymore. Down toward the sea he saw them coming.

One was taller than the rest and he figured it was female. He watched her flitter and in an instant he wanted to lay it all down, shuck flesh and bone, leave the tractor, abandon his tomatoes, the two centuries of his blood in this land and all that held him to the earth, to be fire and wind and thunder, playthings in the hands of God.

But a golf ball ruined it. Hateful and dimpled like a white spider, it rolled through the ferns and rested at his feet. Then he winded her and she smelled like jasmine and he knew she was no ghost. And neither were the others. He saw that a few of them were men, giggling like girls, swinging seven-irons in the moonlight.

# EIGHT

Christy Seabrook was after sheep head, fish that hide under docks and bridges. Low tide was the time to get them, to chum the water with bits of oysters scraped off pilings with an oar blade. Tiny fiddler crabs, herded up on mudflats at low tide, are the best bait – live, impaled on a hook ten feet down at slack water.

Sheep head bite light and fight hard, circling when hooked, trying to cut the line on barnacles lining the dock posts. The striped fish are as big as serving platters and have teeth like wire snips that snap off stainless steel hooks in no time. Slide the bait down the edge of the piling and count to ten and if there's no strike, reel in because the bait's gone.

It can take a hat full of fiddlers to get one sheep head in the boat. But baked or broiled, a sheep head is the finest eating fish in the river, except maybe fresh mullet rolled in cornmeal and fried in bacon grease.

Christy was fishing for sheep head but his mind was on Cap'um Jack's shrimp boat laid up in Bull River four miles away and loaded to the gunnels with Jamaican dope. It was Cap'um Jack's first run for Christy and damn sure his last, the dirty bastard. Ran out of fuel on the way down, out of drinking water on the way back, out of beer at the end. He bored right up Calibogue Sound in broad daylight, dropped anchor in the mouth of Bull River and ran his dingy to Harbour Town to get more beer. Three trucks were waiting on Pine Island; three Donzis were circling the sea buoy. The dirty bastard.

Christy had to pull this deal out of the fire, hold those trucks, bring in the Donzis and re-schedule everything for after sundown. That's why he was not focused on sheep head that day, good as they were.

Christy had more radios in his boat than a fish has scales. AM-FM, a marine-band VHF and a police scanner that could pick up the sheriff, the game wardens and the Coast Guard but not the DEA. He had a walkie-talkie patched in to his crew that was stowed under the seat with the transmit button taped down so every word he spoke went out over the air.

The scanner beeped and squawked. A ship off Savannah requested a harbor pilot; a Yankee yacht somewhere south of Brunswick asked about dockage at Harbour Town Marina; a shrimper off Grenadier Shoals wanted to know the price of diesel at Thunderbolt. Then an officer of the South Carolina Department of Marine Resources said he was about to make a safety inspection. Christy looked out past Pinckney Island where May River dumps into Calibogue Sound and saw the game wardens coming. He turned off the scanner.

They tied up alongside and asked to see his saltwater fishing license. There were two of them wrapped in Kevlar and they toted black automatic pistols. They were not smiling. Christy handed over his boat registration and his fishing license. He held up his life jackets, his foghorn and his box of flares for them to see. "Yes, officer, sir. Thank you, officer, sir."

One life jacket had a broken buckle, and they scowled. They weren't happy about his fire extinguisher, either. The valve was corroded but the pressure gauge needle was still in the green. They wrote him a warning and left.

Christy flipped the scanner back on and in less than fifteen minutes he heard them again, this time telling the dispatcher in Port Royal they were running up Bull River to check out a shrimp boat anchored there.

Shrimpers dropped anchor in Bull River at sundown to sort and ice their catch, then waited for dawn to trawl just off the beach. On summer nights, the battered pine hulls swung on the tide, showing black-lettered names across their sterns: *Captain Ben Lee, Miss Cora Lee, Flying Cloud, Sugar Two* and *Too Fool*. Masts and booms were illuminated by bare bulbs, green nets hung drying over the sides, seabirds roosted on the rigging, Gullah deckhands played bottle-cap checkers while the sun slipped down behind Savannah.

Shrimpers are a tribe of outlaws even when not hauling dope. They shrimp too early and they shrimp too late. They slip into sounds and inlets and trawl in forbidden zones. They let their licenses expire. They refuse to rig attachments to screen out porpoises and sea turtles because it's a lot of trouble setting the devices in the funnels of the nets. Fines levied against recreational fishermen run in the hundreds of dollars, but for a commercial shrimper, it's in the thousands. Wardens seldom cut them slack.

Christy knew that catching violators was not the result of good police investigations or surveillance. It was hit and miss mostly. This time Christy had a skipper MIA on Hilton Head, probably stumbling drunk. He had five million dollars' worth of Bob Marley reefer on a boat in the middle of Bull River at four o'clock in the afternoon and wardens were on the prowl. Christy knew that in his business he must always have a Plan B. He listened to the scanner as the drama unfolded.

Prayer does not come easily to most men and Christy was gratified to hear one of the wardens' spirited invocation: "Great God Almighty, the sumbitch almost rammed us!"

Christy was raised Episcopalian but was not particularly religious. He loved Jesus in a remote sort of way, like He was a distant cousin or something. He loved his fellow man, too, but his fellow women mostly.

"Dispatch, dispatch, we are in hot pursuit. The registration number is..." A blast of static mixed in with the moan of a maxed-out outboard motor broke up the transmission. Then a warden asked, "What was that number? Did you catch the number?"

The boat had a number – they all do – but it had been carefully smeared beyond recognition with river mud. Meanwhile, a sheep head bumped Christy's bait. They bit so light you had to smell them to know they were down there.

"Dispatch, they are headed up Broad Creek!"

Minutes later, the warden barked: "They ran up in the grass! Back-up, back-up! One suspect still in boat, other hauling ass 'cross hard marsh!"

Christy did not hear the details until they got out of jail. The boat blew up Broad Creek full throttle until it ran out of water. One man took off on foot, the other stayed put, and when they put the cuffs on him he whined, "Hell, I just met that guy over at Harbour Town a half-hour ago."

But Christy would hear all of that later. The fish were biting and he had beer and he had ice. *Might as well catch some fish*, he thought, as he waited for sundown.

 # NINE

Yancey sat on the porch and watched the crowd getting off the afternoon ferry. Through fogged old binoculars he saw them move up the gangway and onto the dock: Golfers, birders, tourists, mothers with small children carrying beach toys.

And then he saw her. He recognized her in the way she moved.

He followed her with the glasses, this crown of creation now flesh and bone in broad daylight. He watched the river wind play with her dress and the sunshine fool with her hair. And then he knew – even though he did not know it when he fixated on her on that full-moon fairway – he was in love.

You can take charcoal and scratch big-breasted, round-assed women alongside mastodons, bison and elk on the walls of your cave. You can daub points of red ocher on their tits and trace the lines of their inner thighs. You can dance before them naked and fantasize about what you would do if they were real.

You can fall down in wonder like the Canaanites did and go a-whoring after false gods like so many men still do. You can anoint priestesses and have sex with them on the summer solstice in the great stone temples you build. You can set maidens dancing in the highlands of Kenya and watch them go round and round, their nipples erect, their feet raising dust, their proud flesh bouncing and jiggling and glistening with sweat in the firelight.

You can covet a coven, worship all thirteen at once with your tongue and hands and pelvis. You can waste yourself in bars and bedrooms from Manhattan to New Orleans to Los Angeles, mixing your manhood in a glorious rainbow of femininity. You can write poems, plays, novels and songs. *Be-bop-ba-looba, she's my baby.* But you'll be wasting time.

Yancey was a Baptist and they called him a backslider. Yancey knew better. He ran with loose women because he was tempted more than most men. Yes, he loved his whisky, but mostly drank beer. Yancey knew Jesus was a Jew and He drank wine and not grape juice like the Baptists do. The Egyptians drank beer and Yancey figured Jesus would like that too had Joseph stayed in Egypt long enough for Jesus to reach drinking age. And cuss? Yes, Yancey cussed, but only for good reason.

Yancey knew Bible stories from his childhood and they were in his heart, in his brain. But he always had his own spin:

On the fifth day, the Good Book says, God created all the animals, but not one suited Him. So, on the sixth, God created Adam in His own image. That was a little better, but not much. Then God lined up the fowls of the air and the beasts of the field, the sharks and bass and sheep head of the sea. And He paraded them all by Adam so Adam could give them names.

Adam named them all: The alligators, the mallards, the hippopotami, the obscure species the average man cannot pronounce or spell. The protozoan, the snail darters, the walking fish, the flying fish, the behemoth that dwelleth in the deep. But nowhere in this great flapping, slithering, stomping, squiggling, sloshing melee did Adam find a single creature that suited him.

After naming a couple of hundred thousand of them, Adam was slap worn out. And as Adam slept, God removed one of his ribs, palmed a handful of clay and fashioned a more stylish model, with all the extras. When Adam woke up and found a naked woman lying beside him, he was astounded, as most men are to this day. So Adam looked at Eve and stammered, "Flesh of my flesh, bone of my bone."

Standing there on his front porch, looking through those fogged binoculars at Susan Drake breezing up that dock, Yancey Yarboro felt the rush of the ages rising. Cavemen, Kenyans and Canaanites, but mostly he felt a great kinship with Adam. And he wanted her.

He had a load of groceries on that ferry – ham hocks, smoked neck bones, pork chops and bacon; rice, beans, grits and cornmeal; two cases of beer and a half-gallon of bourbon in a plastic bottle so the deckhands wouldn't bust it when they played soccer with his boxes because Yancey seldom tipped them.

He had called in his order to the Piggly Wiggly and given whoever answered his credit card number. Yancey had a credit card and considered it the Mark of the Beast, the number that Revelations says you must have to buy and sell in the Last Days.

Maybe it was the Last Days already.

His credit card was one of those thousand-dollar models, the kind they send you solicitations for in the mail, saying you're pre-approved when you're really not. They charge twenty-four percent interest, add-ons for overdrafts and late payments so they can make money even if you go defunct after six or seven months. Yancey generally had about two hundred dollars of slack left on it.

It was an expensive way to shop – high interest, long-distance phone calls, twenty bucks to pay somebody at the grocery store to haul his grub to the ferry. But it was cheaper than running his skiff over to Savannah and getting it himself.

The resort bellmen stacked his groceries in the shade and Yancey would wait until they left with baggage for guests at the inn so he would not have to give them a tip. He hooked his trailer behind his tractor and drove over to fetch his vittles home before the meat soured. But that afternoon was different.

He met Susan Drake beneath the spreading oaks at the foot of the dock as he loaded his rations and she struggled with a paper bag packed with wine bottles. The bag was split and when he moved to help her, a bottle of Robert Mondavi Private Selection fell and shattered, throwing shards of glass, splattering vino across her fine-boned feet. The wine was as dark as blood and the pieces of glass shone like emeralds.

There was another Bible story Yancey knew – old King Balthazar's dream about the idol with a head of gold and chest of brass, thighs of iron and feet of clay, and the rock chiseled from the hillside without human hands that rolled down and smashed the idol all to hell. When Daniel told the king what it meant, the king dropped down on his hands and knees and crawled outside, bellowing like a bull and eating grass.

Yancey could have fallen down on his knees and bellowed too as he stood there looking at her. They had been on the island together for years and their paths had not crossed until that moonlit night on the sixth fairway not far from the cassina bushes at the tee box of the seventh. But she lived on the beach and he lived on the back of the island near the river. She was rich and he was poor; she drove an electric golf cart and he drove a faded blue Ford tractor when it worked.

But that did not matter right then. She looked at her feet and he looked at her feet and then they looked at each other face to face.

"Well, ma'am, I reckon I owe you a drink."

"Gin makes me sin," she said.

Yancey saw the diamond on her ring finger and the broad gold band next to it and he said, "Well, ma'am, what rhymes with brown whisky?"

"Frisky," she said.

# TEN

Christy had sheep head for supper. Strange that he would have an appetite, things going halfway to hell like that. But a day in a boat makes a man hungry, even with a five-million-dollar deal under way and the prospect of a dozen years in jail working on his stomach.

He scaled the fish and split it down the backbone, laid it on the grill skin-side down so the fat wouldn't drip into the coals and catch fire. He laid pats of butter here and there on the fish, sprinkled salt, pepper and paprika, and covered it with foil to keep it from drying out. It was done when the butter melted and bubbled and ran.

He sat on his porch and ate it all – the fish, a ladle of grits and the season's first tomatoes. They weren't Yancey's tomatoes. But sliced thick and doctored with soy sauce and red wine vinegar and olive oil, they were good anyway.

Christy had a place now, a condo on the south end of Hilton Head. It was two blocks from the water and had a broad upstairs deck, a rope hammock and a grill overlooking Calibogue Sound, a mile wide and ten miles long, with a deep channel to the sea. Daufuskie Island – high, green, heavy-timbered – was on the far side. The headwaters of Calibogue divided, then divided again into a filigree of rivers and little creeks, many of them with deepwater docks.

Pine Island was out there too, just perfect for off-loading marijuana, especially with Mike McElvern watching over things. Christy was happy to have struck a deal with his high school classmate. Christy had skipped college and run off and got psychedelic. But they shared a history and a culture. There was not a lot of explaining between them when they talked. In that way, they were like brothers.

Christy wished he had ten men like Mike working for him. But instead he was stuck with a parade of characters including Cap'um Jack – the dirty bastard – and plagues of yellow-eyed Jamaicans, indifferent Panamanians and half-breed Hondurans outstanding only in incompetence, clever only in treachery. All sat, rolled over and were forever for sale to the highest bidder, whether it was for more money or reduced time. Christy dreaded working with them.

Mike held the trucks and turned the stevedores loose and gave them enough to keep them quiet but not enough to keep them from coming back: Five thousand dollars each for five hours work. He had dredged them up from the last-gasp crowd at Mudbank Mammy's, a concrete-floor beer joint on Johnson Creek where the barmaids swept up the eyeballs at closing time.

Christy rescheduled the Donzis to get the dope off the *Lucky J* and onto the dock at Pine Island after dark. Mike got it into three rented vans and sent one off to Atlanta, one to Richmond and the other to Charlotte.

It was a long night but Christy came home with a suitcase full of fifties and hundreds. He figured Cap'um Jack would soon come looking for his share and he had to keep Cap'um Jack happy to shut him up. But just the thought of giving him anything galled Christy. So he peeled off twenty thousand and some change, double-wrapped the rest in garbage bags and stuffed them into the pine-straw mulch under the azalea bushes by the front door of his condo. As the sun slipped away, he headed out for one last chore.

Mike, grim-faced, met Christy at the dock. "You got my money?" he asked.

The tide was three hours into flood and the water sucked and gurgled around the pilings. "You bring that crab bait?" Christy asked.

Mike pointed to the skiff, rocking against the float, nudging at the lines in the river's flow. The wire-bound box of baitfish was past rank, oozing and drawing flies. "I didn't figure you a crabber," he said.

Christy started to say something about crab pots and pot, but the pun wouldn't quite come together, so he simply smiled, stepped on board and fired the engine. Mike dropped the stern line, moved up and stood astride the dock cleat. He held out his hand, rubbed his index finger with his thumb like he wanted some cash. Christy eased the boat into gear, held her against a tide so swift you could not swim against it. "OK. OK. Drop that line and jump aboard," he said. "I got your money and I got more."

The *Lucky J* was anchored in a cove in a river bend where the current cut deep into the outside bank. At high tide the boat was almost hidden against the tree line; at low water, invisible. Shorebirds and seabirds, gulls and pelicans took wing, screaming outrage as Christy and Mike pulled alongside in the dying light. Blue herons flapped off dejectedly to roost in the pines.

"Thought you already handled this," Mike said.

"I wish," Christy sighed. "It's just like every other damn thing. Got to stay on it to get it right."

The crew had sprayed the deck with fifteen hundred pounds of pressure hose, blowing all the seeds and stems and dust overboard. The planks were still slick with Dove dishwashing detergent – the only kind that lathered in salt water. Christy swung his legs over the gunnels and climbed aboard the shrimp boat. Mike followed, lugging the box of bait.

"Damn, this is getting ripe," Mike sniffled. "Where you want it?"

Christy waved toward the stern. "Just open her up and set her on the deck back there."

"Birds will spread it all over," Mike said.

"Exactly. Deck's too clean. Tomorrow it'll be slobbered with fish heads and bird shit."

"Damn, Christy, you think of everything."

Christy slid back a hatch cover and peered below. "That's what I get paid for," he said over his shoulder. "Hand me the flashlight."

Mike peeled the lid off the bait and wired it open. "Where's the light?"

"In my boat bag. Grab that radio, too."

Mike scrambled into the skiff and came back with the bag. He passed Christy the flashlight and puzzled over the scanner. "How you work this thing?"

"Just turn it on. It's all set."

Christy moved the beam back and forth in the darkened hold. Even in the cool of the afternoon, the air down there reeked of reefer. "We got to go over every inch of this boat. Chuck a couple of fish down here."

A handful of mullet splattered into the darkness.

"Jack stiffed you. Why you doing this for him?"

"If he gets busted," Christy said, "we might, too."

"We?" Mike asked.

"We," Christy replied.

"This like working for the CIA? I got to die to quit?"

"You making money. Why quit?"

"I ain't seen no money."

Christy grinned and patted his shirt pocket.

They were below decks now, duck-walking forward around the engine and the gearbox and over the chain that drives the winches. It smelled good down there – the reefer, diesel fuel, gear lube, bilge, lines and pitch sweating out the Georgia pine hull. In the old days, they built boats like this along the riverbanks, a crew of Gullah carpenters hewing ribs from the curved limbs of great oaks. They laid the bottoms and covered them in copper and drove oakum between the planks as the hull rose higher and higher above the keel. They filled the air with Gullah talk, a lazy-sounding patois of bondage, blues and voodoo, while they littered the ground with pine shavings and wisps of oakum and crushed Prince Albert tobacco cans and tattered wrappers of B-C Headache Powders and shards from the bottles of whisky they drank every Friday afternoon.

They had no written plans. The boats were forty, fifty, sixty feet, but they looked much the same – sharp prows, swells along the gunnels as smooth as female hips, sterns low enough for the nets to come aboard, high enough to keep the sea off the rear decks. The pilot houses were cypress, way forward with plenty of room for machinery behind. The engines were government surplus, diesels mostly but sometimes gas, and the stuffing boxes and rudderposts and cleats came from Savannah before the River Street ship chandlers sold out to restaurants and clip joints.

But the old-time boat builders have crossed their last river, and steel-hulled seagoing trawlers with names like *Kim Sea King* and *Saigon Warrior* take most of the catch now. You can hear the Koreans and Vietnamese jabber on the radio and have no idea what they're catching or where.

Meanwhile, Christy was doing what he could to keep another local shrimper in business for another year, even though Cap'um Jack did not deserve it, the dirty bastard.

They were out of the engine room and under the wheelhouse when Mike asked, "You want some fish down here, too?"

Christy followed his nose to a forward compartment, stowage for extra lines and spare anchor and chain. He wrenched open the door and started cussing. Back topside again, with the light failing and brown velvet dark creeping across woods, sky and water, Mike and Christy wrestled big bags of reefer down into the skiff.

"I didn't sign up for this shit," Mike said.

Christy took another burlap bag and stashed it under the forward seat. "Me neither. But what else can we do?"

"There goes that *we* shit again."

Two bags later Christy said, "Mike, I want you to stick with me for a while."

"I reckon you do," Mike said, taking a swipe at the evening's first mosquito. "You'd play hell moving five hundred pounds by yourself."

The skiff was riding low in the water now. "Four hundred and forty," Christy said. "That's twenty ten-kilo bags."

"Whatever," Mike grunted. "Here's the one I was looking for."

"Which one?" Christy asked.

"The last one of these sumbitches."

Christy grinned. "Cast off and jump in."

They idled off into the night with the *Lucky J* fading into the darkness below the tree line, into the shadows of time when there would be no more boats like this.

"Where we taking it?" Mike asked.

Christy nipped one of the bags with his jackknife. He peeled out a bud, as green and as hard and as big as a flashlight battery. He tossed Mike the bud and a pack of rolling papers. "Spin one."

"Where we taking it?" Mike asked again.

"Don't worry," Christy said. "To a place they'll never find."

ELEVEN

Yancey Yarboro had a date with Susan Drake.

Not really.

She asked him to stop by the inn Friday evening. She said she was meeting a few friends at seven and either she would buy him a drink or he could buy her one. He forgot which.

It did not matter.

Asking Yancey how many women he had bedded in his lifetime was like asking him how many deer he had killed. He would have to get off by himself and puzzle over it for a spell. Does a boat count as a bed? How about a horse trailer? Or a pile of busted tomato crates? He might not know the exact number but he remembered a little of each and how all were beautiful for a moment and no two were quite the same.

But Susan Drake scared him. She was a looker, Lord knows, and the poetry welled up inside him whenever he thought about her. And something else worried him about her but he didn't know exactly what it was. Maybe it was the way she moved, her grace. Maybe it was something he saw in her on the seventh tee, or the jasmine perfume and a north-Georgia twang that drew two syllables each from *gin* and *sin*. He could see it, smell it, hear it, but he could not name it, and it scared the hell out of him.

The heart wants what the heart wants and no sense can be made of it.

But it was only Wednesday and he had to talk face-to-face with the Judge about those damn survey stakes. The Judge was Yancey's daddy and Yancey had not seen him a dozen times in a dozen years and this left a great big hole in Yancey's heart.

The Judge gave Yancey his life, and thirty years later he gave him his life again when the burglars held him at knifepoint, and Yancey, who survived twenty months in combat, could not do a thing.

"Take us to your daddy," one of them hissed into his ear.

They were dressed in black and wore masks and carried Fairborne fighting knives, which Yancey had seen before, though he wished he had not. One grabbed him by his hair and cold steel burned the flesh of his throat. The other held a blade at the base of Yancey's skull as they bundled him down the hall.

It was a long walk to the Judge's bedroom door.

Yancey had come with the annual rent, thirteen thousand dollars, one-third the revenue from his crop, a fine year for tomatoes. He and the Judge got into the sour mash, as usual, before the old man wobbled off to bed. Yancey, too drunk for either the highway or the waterway, crawled into his boyhood bed and dreamed golden dreams of youthful days on the river.

He dreamed it was Christmas when the Judge had left him a new cypress skiff pulled up beneath the oaks along the marsh. His father had freed a black boatwright and the skiff was a token of gratitude, as they say. The boat was twelve feet long and had no place for a motor, but she was so slick and so light she could almost plane with the oars.

So Yancey plied the river at the age most boys pedaled bikes. Riding tide and wind, poling through the marsh, rowing into the creek and across the sound, camping, hunting and fishing made a man of him.

But the dream became a nightmare. The enemy had him by the hair. The blade across his throat and the one at the back of his neck were real. There was a light in the hall just outside his daddy's door. Yancey knocked and the Judge said, "What the hell you want, boy?"

And Yancey said, "Daddy, two men are here and they want to, uh, talk to you."

After ten seconds of waiting at the gates of hell, the Judge said, "Well, open the goddamn door."

The Judge kept a loaded Police Positive .38 on his bedside table, a gun like the cops carried in the 1930s. Six shots, a six-inch barrel, a gift from a deputy cleared of drunken driving. It shot straight if you knew how to handle it.

Drunk or sober, the Judge knew how. He could drop a deer on the run and a quail on the wing, and he could dust three clay pigeons right out of the air – *pap, pap, pap* – with that pistol.

Yancey knew what was coming.

The first man got it between the eyes; the second had just enough time to turn his head. He got it in the temple. Blood and brains splattered the floor and walls.

The Judge called Sheriff Wallace at home. Yancey shuffled down to the riverbank and thought of his boyhood boat while he waited. The sheriff came quickly, along with Coroner Pinckney. Wallace was a retired highway cop with no stomach for blood, but Pinckney was so tough he could put his plate on a dead man's face and eat supper. The men powwowed on the porch while the deputies snapped pictures, bagged the bodies and loaded them into the hearse. No lights, no siren.

Yancey went back inside and mopped the floor. Human blood was like pig blood, deer blood. It did not bother him much. But the brains were like cottage cheese and blueberries and Yancey never ate either again.

Coroner Pinckney bound Yancey's father over on two counts of first-degree murder so nobody could say he showed favoritism to an old friend. Another judge released him on his own recognizance. Six months later the grand jury ruled it self-defense and everything was quiet until the phone started ringing.

It would have made sense if the victims had been crackheads from Savannah who would happily kill anybody for loose change. But they weren't from Savannah. They were U.S. Marines, instructors at the nearby Parris Island rifle range. They were Yankee boys, Jarheads. No criminal records, lots of commendations. The families were convinced the Judge and the Sheriff and the Coroner were in cahoots, that they conspired to kill their boys for some reason. The Marine Corps looked into the matter and decided that the minute those men took those government knives off the base, they were no longer U.S. Marines.

That's when persons unknown started calling – midnight, two in the morning, sunrise – from a pay phone in a small town in upstate Michigan, the records showed. They threatened the Judge and the Sheriff and the Coroner, but that wasn't good enough. So they called the reporters.

The Charleston newspaper ran an article on the first anniversary of the shooting, "Old Case, New Questions." Was it really a random robbery?

Everybody had an opinion: Wrong house. Contract killing. Bribes. Dope. Somebody said it was Yancey they were after, not the Judge. The papers kept at it until the Judge took early retirement. Yancey let it drop. He tried to talk to his daddy about what had happened, but the words hung up in his throat like dry grits.

Yancey dreamed about it – not the flashes of gunfire, not the double thunderclap and not the bloody brains, but about a logical explanation. He dreamed that he and the Judge were walking along the beach at low tide, with the water frothing at their bare feet. He was a child again and his daddy was wearing his black robe the way he did when Yancey was a boy. "Daddy, none of this makes sense," he said looking straight into his father's eyes. The Judge offered an explanation that made perfect sense in a world where the river always runs, the tide always changes and porpoises blow just beyond the surf, their breath hanging in the air like salty geysers. By morning, Yancey could not remember what his father had said.

Yancey was not Old King Balthazar. He had no Daniel to call on to sort out his dreams. After a year or two the dreams dwindled to nothing, but the question weighed heavy on his heart. So Yancey stayed on Daufuskie, worked the fields, drank his whisky, and loved his women and hoped they loved him back. The Judge settled for whisky.

For both his daddy and his momma, whisky was a luxury they could afford when they were the bright young attorney and the pretty little wife, and later the Honorable Clarence H. Yarboro and his still-pretty but slightly lush wife. But age, liquor and loneliness caught up with them. Now Yancey's momma slept till noon and only left the house a couple of times a month for groceries and booze. As for the Judge, he stayed public for a year or so, showing up and shaking hands, but then his weekly excursions regularly resulted in "incidents." He would be escorted home by a cop or a concerned citizen, a practice that was curtailed after what the newspaper described as "an assault upon an officer of the law while in his underwear."

You had to read the article carefully to learn whether it was the cop or the Judge who was in his underwear. When Yancey dared broach the subject, the Judge snapped, "It was my bathing suit, goddamnit!"

Now Yancey must talk to him about those survey stakes, so he was getting everything ready to cross the river.

TWELVE

"You can't bring that damn thing in here!" the man at the front gate said. He was a Daufuskie Island Club and Resort security guard, one of three who intermittently manned the entrance. Half the time nobody was there. You could breeze right through and drive around the place like you owned it until somebody called and the guards came.

This one was pushing sixty and overweight and the skeeters swarmed in a great cloud around his head. He looked like a British colonial officer – khakis, epaulets and a white pith helmet. "What in the hell are you thinking?" the man snapped.

Yancey's tractor rattled and smoked but kept on running. "Well, how in the hell you expect me to get there?"

The guard crossed his arms and rocked on his heels and stuck out his belly, which strained the lower buttons of his shirt. He did not hold the pose long. The bugs had him twitching, swatting and scratching. "Do I know you?"

"Yeah, I'm Yancey Yarboro, the guy with the tomato fields ..." He was about to add, "that some son-of-a-bitch stuck survey stakes all over," but did not.

The guard swiped at his ears, fanned the back of his neck. "Mr. Yarboro you know this is a private community for the exclusive use of members and guests."

Yarboros had been on Daufuskie long before security guards arrived. Yancey roamed this place as a boy, shooting squirrels, rabbits and deer. His first deer was a spike buck, and killing it was easier than he thought it would be. It slipped into the acorns a little after four one December afternoon when the surf looked like glycerin and the sea fog blanketed all creation. The buck saw Yancey first and they stared at each other for longer than Yancey could stand. Yancey trembled and shook but the buck didn't care and when he dipped his head for one last mouthful of acorns, Yancey got him in the sights.

And there was the wild turkey the day before Easter that he slung over his shoulder and toted home to his momma. It was not as good as a store-bought bird, if you like a store-bought bird. It had no plastic pop-up timer. It was all dark meat and the thighs and back fell apart with only a fork at supper. That was when no gates were on the island, when it was all swamp and trees, when the red-brick chimneys of the Daufuskie Island big house stood sad and silent in the pines before they hauled them off to make sidewalks for the inn.

"I been invited," Yancey explained. "Reckon that makes me a guest."

The guard went into the shack and came out with a clipboard and a pen. He was not smart enough to be sarcastic and it takes no intelligence to take offense. He began scratching with his pencil. "Who is your host tonight?"

"Susan Drake."

The pencil stopped scratching. "Mrs. Drake?"

"Yep," said Yancey, who wanted to choke him for the way he said it.

"OK," the guard said, fanning through the papers. "Let's see, it's wrote down here somewhere."

Yancey hit the clutch and ground the tractor into gear.

"But you can't take that damn thing in there! Only electric carts or horse-drawn conveyances."

"Horse-drawn conveyances?"

"We maintain a stable for the use of our members and guests."

Yancey turned his tractor around and left. It was two miles to Gator Brown's house. Yancey drove the darkened roads and there is no place so dark as Daufuskie Island before the moon comes up. It was the third quarter and it would not come up till after midnight. Meanwhile, Yancey thought about the time he had crossed the river to talk to the Judge.

It was not a bad run in good weather, about a dozen miles, much of it on sheltered rivers and creeks. But Calibogue Sound was right in the middle – deep, blue, wide and dangerous, like a two-hearted woman, a simile that came easy to Yancey. There was an east wind and an ebb tide and some wicked rollers in the Sound. Yancey had not worn his slicker since the tropical storm blew ashore last time. He had wandered around the house trying to remember where he left it.

If you did not know this man by his face and by his heart, you would know him by his home and by his stuff: The handmade cast net in a plastic bucket by the door, seven fishing rods piled in the corner, an old shotgun on the heart-pine mantel alongside the box-framed Purple Heart and Expert Rifleman badges on green felt backing. The walls were covered with photos of old hunters, dogs and guns. There was a flyspecked "Jesus Bless This Home" sign and empty Red Stripe bottles on a battered wooden table. There was a bed, always unmade, and you could see from the sweat-stained sheets which side he slept on.

There was one single room with a large closet for a toilet and shower, and a rickety back stoop. It had a broad front screen porch with a view of the river that a million bucks couldn't buy, and a rusty tin roof that rattled you to sleep in the rain. The sidewalk of rough brick led to a backyard jungle of azaleas and camellias that needed pruning and a shed for the tractor, the extra outboard motor, sacks of duck decoys and a pile of tomato crates.

Yancey would not have traded any of it for a white-columned plantation house, even if somebody else paid the taxes. Yancey never paid his taxes on time because the penalties were less than the interest on money he would have had to borrow to pay them. He had a deal with the Judge – one-third the value of the crop, which Yancey always paid, and keep the land taxes current, which often he did not. The sheriff could sell the land after three years and some legal work and then Yancey had another year to redeem it if he paid in full plus some swindle fees at the last minute. Still it was less than the interest on borrowed money.

It happened that Yancey was two years behind and expected a new tax statement in the mail any day now. This was not a good thing, apt to send the Judge into a blizzard of cussing if he found out. Neither was it a thing to be thinking about when crossing big water where a man needed to pay attention lest he wind up in fine print on the obituary page of the Beaufort Gazette.

These rivers are beautiful but deadly and the list of names of those who went down to them and never came back is a long one. Countless swamped and holed boats had blown up on the beaches, and empty life jackets, or life jackets with bloated bodies in them – face-down, noses, lips and ears nibbled off by crabs and fish.

Yancey was a farmer and he loved the feel of moist dirt in his hands and to sniff its musk. But he was also a waterman without peer, a river dog, which is as fine a compliment as you can get down here. He went up the Cooper River to where the channel played out in a great swaying bed of spartina, where spot-tail bass lolled in the shallows, and shrimp and barnacles crackled at the tide change. Then he headed down to Bull River where the *Lucky J* still swung at anchor. Yancey knew a good boat when he saw one and the *Lucky J* was as good as they come. It had been there a week now and he wondered about it as he spun down river, picturing the pilot house windows and gunnels splattered with broad white guano drippings. Yancey had beached his skiff at Lubkin's Seafood and tethered it to a skinny oak in case he didn't get back until after the tide change. It had another couple of hours of ebb left to go and two hours into the flood; the boat would float again, which meant four hours to do business with the Judge.

Yancey's pickup was parked across the road in the shade. It wasn't much of a truck, rusty around the fenders and old enough to vote. But the tires held air even if the radiator leaked, and generally the rig started if it hadn't sat too long. Since it often did sit a week or two at a time, Yancey left the windows rolled up tight to keep out snakes and spiders. It had been nearly a week and was hot as an oven inside. Yancey opened the doors to let it air out while he went to find Meatball Jenkins.

Meatball sold boat gas from an ancient pump down on the dock. It was cheaper than car gas since it did not have state road tax factored into the price. If you filled up a jerry can and dumped it in your truck, Meatball wouldn't give a damn and you could save fourteen cents a gallon. It wasn't much, but after six months or so, you'd have saved enough to buy a case of beer.

Yancey was lugging the gas can back to his truck when a station wagon wheeled around the corner in a great cloud of dust. On top was a man clinging to the roof rack. He was wearing pajamas.

"Great God A-mighty," Meatball said. "Here come de Judge."

Yancey's momma locked up the brakes when she saw her son. The Judge fixed him with one bloodshot eye and an idiotic grin. "Why hello, boy."

Yancey bent down and looked his momma square in the face. "Do you know Daddy's hanging on the roof?"

Yancey's mother bore a hint of her former beauty, but only a hint. Her lips were full and red but her cheeks were a sunken spider web of pink and purple. Day or night, she never left the house without wearing dark glasses.

"Hell yes," she said. "He won't ride with me 'cause I'm drunk."

"He pilot light be flick'rin'," Meatball Jenkins added.

# THIRTEEN

Gator Brown's dog met Yancey at the front steps. He was a three-legged, one-eyed mongrel – yellow, skinny, whip-tailed and sharp-nosed. His ears had big notches scalloped from the edges. If you took every dog in the world and let them breed as they would and fed the pups half what they needed, in a hundred years you would have a dog like this. Gator Brown's hound was like most of the other island dogs, except for his missing parts.

Over the years, Gator Brown had owned a long string of yellow dogs, most in about the same shape. This is how he got his name. He would chain whatever dog he had at the time just outside an alligator burrow, ease back a few yards and sit down. When the dog got lonesome and his yipping and howling fetched up the reptile, Gator Brown would stick a load of buckshot in his gun. A gator is as fast as a horse for the first thirty feet. They bow, head and tail held high, and get up on their feet and move. Gator Brown's latest dog was named Popeye. Yancey called him Lucky.

Even though Gator Brown did not hunt much anymore, he kept the dog anyway. He was getting up in years and besides the government had taken all the profit out of gator hunting by fining the hell out of anybody caught with the hides. Gator tail is a mild-tasting fine white meat, a bit chewy but as good as gopher turtle or rattlesnake.

But a man can consume only so much gator tail. The money was in the hides and since it was worrisome to think about the possibility of getting bit and busted at the same time, nobody hunted them much anymore.

And now the gators are so thick in summertime you don't dare walk out beside freshwater after dark, or saltwater either during dry years when the beasts take to whatever water they can find. If a gator gets too uppity, somebody's likely to nail him, but that's not often. During the March and April breeding season, when the bulls get restless and the females protective of their new nests, the Yankee tourists are advised to keep a close eye on their kids.

Lucky didn't take much stock in white folks. He was the kind of dog who would slip up behind one and grab him about halfway up the calf, or if the fleas and ticks had him dizzy and his worms and arthritis were bothering him and he just didn't feel like reaching, he'd bite him clean through the heel above the line of his shoe.

A dog bite hurts more than you think, especially when an island mongrel gets a hold of you. They must have gotten something from the very soil of this place, like the copperheads and the bugs do, whatever makes their bites worse than ones you get elsewhere. But Lucky knew Yancey, so he let him onto the porch.

The house was dark except for a single candle flame dancing through the dirty glass of the parlor window. Yancey rapped on the door.

"Come on in, Mr. Yance," Gator Brown said.

Yancey stepped inside the shanty. It was a lot like his own place, but not as big, not as clean. "How'd you know it was me?" Yancey asked.

Gator Brown sat at the table with a swath of papers laid out next to a little statue of Jesus, like the kind Catholics glue to the dashboards of their cars. Also on the table were a homemade whisk broom made of herbs tied up with a twist of twine, a sprinkling of dirt, a couple of seashells and a black candle. Gator Brown held the candle on its side and hot wax splattered onto the papers – *drip, drip, drip* – blotting out the text one phrase at a time. "Who else drive a Fode?" he asked. "Who else get by Popeye?"

"Gator Brown, what in the world you doing?"

Gator Brown held up his hand. "Shhh. Set yo'self down, Mr. Yance. I be done directly."

Yancey pulled up a chair and watched. Gator Brown mumbled a few words that Yancey did not catch. He sat the butt of the candle into a pool of hot wax and held it until it stuck, then got up and hobbled into the kitchen. He came back with a can of Red Devil lye, the kind you dump down a clogged toilet. Yancey noticed the papers were the annual county tax statements. He could not read the numbers but he knew his were waiting for him at the island post office and his numbers were likely a damn sight bigger than Gator's, and it troubled him.

Gator Brown levered open the can with a tarnished and twisted spoon, sprinkled lye over the papers and the pooled wax. Then he pressed the lid back onto the can and dusted the papers with a pinch of dirt and swept it all around with the little broom. Then he rolled the papers up around the shells and the broom and rubbed his hands together. "Bury 'um in de ya'd," he said, "out by de gate pos'."

"That gonna work?" Yancey asked.

Gator Brown leaned back in his chair and grinned. "Sump'in gwine happ'n," he said with the utmost certainty.

"Whass-dat?" Yancey asked, getting into the rhythm. Yancey switched to Gullah from time to time and he could speak it pretty good, but not nearly as good as he'd like. Sometimes he figured the person he was talking to might resent his imperfections, but once you hear Gullah and come to love it, you'll forever want to speak it. This evening the words rolled off his tongue like a Bull River oyster on the half shell. Lordy, it tasted good. "De tax man, he head turn 'round back-ard 'n' he walk on down de skreet barkin' like ol' Popeye?"

Gator Brown shrugged and grinned. "I ain' know, but sump'in always happen. Jus' wait, Mr. Yance, jus' wait 'n' see." He paused a second or two, and then cut a sly smile. "Looky here, why you out roamin' in de dark? Likka o' wimmens?"

"Gator Brown," Yancey said, leaning across the table, "can I borry dat mule?"

"Henrietta Fode? Boy, you finally gettin' some sense." He rose from his chair. "I harness she up."

"Set back down, Gator Brown, I jus' want Henrietta."

"Why sho'. But ain' got no saddle."

"I can ride bareback."

"I know dat."

Gator Brown sat back down and held his hand a little higher than the top of the table. "I seen you ride since you dis high, tearin' down de rode on yo' pony. But can't spote no gal on no mule. You needs a wagon wid a hank of hay throwed in the back." Gator Brown actually said *shrowed*, but if you wrote like he talked, nobody would understand it. "Gal might like that bony-back ol' mule mo' dan she like you."

"I ain' say nuttin' 'bout no gal," Yancey said.

"You ain' haf to, boy. Be on yo' face."

Yancey had trouble figuring out how Gator Brown knew all he knew, why the Mexicans crossed themselves and said *brujo* when they saw the old man ambling up the road.

Yancey had a history teacher in high school who said they stripped slaves naked and hauled them across the ocean without anything but a swatch of rough cloth wrapped around their private parts. But that was a lie like a lot of other things they lied about back then. The slaves brought watermelon seeds in their ears and okra seeds in their hair and so much love in their hearts that it filled up the South with compassion from Richmond clear down to New Orleans. They brought recipes they had memorized – the ways to weave cast nets and sweetgrass baskets. They brought singing from the soul, and they brought *ju-ju*, too.

You could talk about cooking, watermelon, okra, nets, baskets and soulful singing any time, but you'd best go easy with the *ju-ju*. Down in Haiti it's called *voudoun* and in New Orleans it's *voodoo*. On the South Carolina Sea Islands, that kind of magic is too fearsome for anybody's lips. But here Yancey was, asking to borrow a mule to get to a girl who lived behind security gates, and there Gator Brown was, bringing the wrath of Mother Africa down upon the duly constituted county government. So Yancey had to say something.

"You just sit here, Gator Brown, with that *ju-ju*, and throw some my way while I get the bridle. I'll have her home by dayclean."

"Just turn 'um loose when dat gal done wid you. She know de way home."

"Turn loose de gal or de mule?" Yancey asked.

"Turn all bofe 'um loose, Mr. Yance. I reckon dat gal know de way home, too."

"How old that mule, Gator Brown?"

"Gettin' up dere. She de mule dat carry Lord Jesus to Jerusalem."

Yancey laughed. "Gator Brown, that weren't no mule! That a jackass!"

Gator Brown snorted. "How you talk, boy? Jesus wouldn't truck wid no jackass."

"Uh-uh, Gator Brown. I know. I been to Sunday school befo'."

Gator Brown looked at him and shook his head sadly. "You go, but you ain' liss'um. Bible say He ride on de foal of de ass. Dat what Henrietta be."

Yancey shook his head. A mule is the foal of a horse that had been bred to a jackass, not the other way around. But it didn't matter. Gator Brown said Jesus rode a mule and that was that. "Gator Brown, dey ain' no arg'ing wid you!"

"Dat right, boy. Don' you dispute wid Gator Brown. He know what he know."

Gator Brown walked his guest out the door and onto the porch. Yancey was halfway to the barn when he heard Gator Brown holler.

"Watch out, boy, dat stuff kill mo' men than likka and dope ta'gedda!"

FOURTEEN

Susan Drake waited for Yancey Yarboro in the clubhouse lounge, wondering why she gave a damn. She had called the front gate so he'd have no trouble getting in. It was a quarter past eight and the wind was off the sea and he wasn't there yet.

Lord knows it had been a long time, way too long, since she had a real man. Despite Poogey Drake's numerous indiscretions and unending excesses, she had been a faithful wife.

Well, almost. There was the time over on Hilton Head at the piano bar. The man could play jazz, especially Gershwin, and she almost wished she could remember his name. He was drunk and wearing a tux and she was drunk and showing her tits. He tore up the score from *Porgy and Bess,* and stared at her all through "A Woman is a Sometime Thing."

So she did him on the beach, dress pulled up, top pulled down. The next day she felt like she'd been buffed with a wire brush. "Damn, damn, I've caught something for sure," she said to herself.

She worried herself into a migraine, called up WebMD online and ran down the long list of possibilities. But in a couple of days she healed and knew, bad as it was, it was only sand.

And there was the man Poogey hired to look after the yard. She lay naked on the couch one morning and when she looked up and saw him staring at her through the patio door, she did not cover herself. He stood there looking at her with his hand on his crotch in the late morning light. That excited her more than you can imagine and she could tell the feeling was mutual. But later when she got to worrying about it, she told Poogey she had caught the man peeking at her when she came from the shower. It was almost true. Poogey fired him and took her to bed and tried to possess her again. It was not good enough.

She wondered if the yardman might return, which would have been fine with her. She thought about it when she soaped herself in the shower, about him slipping up behind her when water was in her eyes. And he would put his hand over her mouth and she'd bite his hand and ...

But he did not come back. Now she waited for Yancey Yarboro. It was like she had three women penned up inside her, penned up tight and snarling and snapping at each other. Sometimes when the moon was up and the surf was high she would lie in bed and think about them, even name them: Nicki and Twyla and Sunny, perhaps. But if she ever did that, she might talk to them and they might talk to each other and leave her out of the conversation. So she decided to leave those bitches alone.

Susan Drake liked pills and she liked doctors, especially rich good-looking ones. But she never wanted to get like those other women who took pills. They did not jump when a door slammed and were so damned sweet all the time. So she laid off the pills and talked to herself often, reciting mantras of many things to do when she was happy, and mild and muted profanities when she was not. Now she quietly cursed herself, wondering why she was waiting for this man.

He was tanned and muscled, wild about the eyes, and he moved with a confidence that did not require a thousand-dollar suit. His eyes were the color of the sky after it rained and a fire welled up inside her when she thought of him.

A lot of men – more men than she could remember – courted her shamelessly because they knew Poogey was no saint. They corralled her at parties, trailed her outside to smoke, brought her drinks. Some were cute and rich. She twittered and glowed whenever they were around, casually touching them about the hands and arms while engaging them in conversation. This drove them delirious with lust, but she never really gave a damn. This farmer, however, this Yancey Yarboro, was not like the rest, and she almost hated him for it.

She didn't wait alone. Jimmie and Johnny and Chip and Cassandra and Sherida flitted and hovered like bees round their queen, as they should, since Susan always picked up the tab. At the last minute she invited them to join her, figuring to gang up on this wild man and dilute the pheromones. If he were a no-show, she'd still have her friends.

Chip came back from the bar with his third martini. Dry or sweet, clean or dirty, vodka or gin, he was unburdened by any great prejudice regarding martinis. Susan had bought her friends various trifles through the years and it was never hard to find something for Chip – the electric clock with each hour marked with a martini glass, the framed cartoons of young men bound up in muscles and chains, colognes she grabbed on jaunts around the world, and the cute little leather mask that when laced up tight in the back covered his face so tight he could not scream.

Chip was insufferable sober and intolerable drunk, but in between, he was charming. Being gay was not easy, but not as difficult as it used to be in South Carolina. He passed Cassandra on her way back for her fourth pink gin, gave her a little squeeze on the ass and a peck on the cheek. She wiggled and rubbed her considerable breasts along his arm.

When Chip sat down next to Susan, he was all-girl again. "Honey," he said, leaning toward her ear, "who *are* you expecting tonight?"

"Her husband," Sherida said with a wink and a nod, a giggle and shrug.

This provoked the usual round of jokes about her status as a single married woman and Jimmie said he was going to buy her a pair of reading glasses since doing what she was doing would slowly drive her blind. She chuckled and patted his cheek as Johnny gazed across the room in rapture. "My, my," he purred, "ain't he a rugged thing."

# FIFTEEN

Yancey had looked in the mirror enough times to know he wasn't much to look at. A run of acne at fifteen pitted the skin that stretched across his cheekbones. He fell off a chair and busted his nose when he was three, then again at thirty-three when he pulled on a wrench when he should have pushed. He sunburned easily and from May to September his nose looked like it had a run-in with a belt sander. But women liked him anyway.

He could spot one, smell her essence, and get her if he kept at it. Yancey loved Jesus and figured Jesus didn't approve, so he prayed occasionally for deliverance, and forgiveness, too, in case he wasn't delivered on time. Now Yancey was in the thick of it again and Jesus was nowhere in sight.

The lounge looked like an English gentlemen's club where men gathered to sip fine whisky and discuss the Zulu War. But dust was on the glasses. The mirror behind the bar was cracked. The backing showed through the carpet near the door and women were allowed.

Three of them, blonde and busty, stood looking at Yancey, but Susan Drake was the real thing – the nails, the hair, the clothes from Saks. He had never been inside a Saks Fifth Avenue store, didn't know what kind of woman shopped there, but he guessed it would be women like Susan Drake.

Why in the hell did she call? he wondered.

He didn't know what to make of one of the men, but the other two appeared to be aging models in a Panama Jack clothing ad – vaguely masculine, mostly good-looking. Susan smiled as he sauntered over to their table.

Yancey could feel mule sweat through his jeans and his legs ached from the ride. "If I ever get ahead in the tomato business, I'm going to buy me a horse so I won't have no bullshit at the gate," he muttered to himself. A moon buzz was working on him even though it was already into its third quarter. Maybe the buzz wasn't lunar this time.

Susan took his hands into hers and cooed, "How so very nice."

She had good hands, long thin fingers, full strong palms. Her red nails matched her lipstick and were neatly manicured, except for a few chips where she bit them. He looked directly into her eyes again and said, "The pleasure is mine, ma'am."

He wondered if she could hear his pulse chugging like a one-cylinder German diesel that Yankee skippers use for motor sailing.

Susan laughed low and throaty, cured by cigarettes and honed on whisky. They eyed each other long enough for everyone to notice.

"My friends," she finally said. "Mr. Yancey Yarboro."

The women rose to meet him, but only one of the men bothered. Yancey shook his hand first.

"I'm Johnny," the man said.

Yancey hugged each of the ladies. One was a little taller than the other, but neither was as tall as Susan Drake.

"Sherida," the shorter one said.

"Cassandra," said the other as she pressed her breasts against Yancey's left arm.

Yancey figured Sherida had been called Sheri too many times, so he named her Miss Reeda instead. Cassandra was Miss Cassie.

He leaned across the table and shook Jimmie's hand. Yancey did not like Jimmie so he didn't call him anything.

"Call me Chip," the little man chirped, "or call me anything. Just call me."

Miss Reeda was charming, conversational. Miss Cassie was all over him. They sat down together. Yancey was squeezed between Miss Reeda and Miss Cassie, and Chip sat beside Susan Drake. Susan stroked the inside of Chip's thigh while Yancey talked about the weather, tomatoes and blossom rot.

Miss Reeda wanted to know if he really did live on Daufuskie, and when he said he did, Miss Cassie asked what he did when he needed a woman. Yancey said he got by as best as he could, and when Susan asked how his luck was running lately, he said it was too soon to tell.

He talked about what fish were biting and they talked about golf and Yancey realized all of them were in on the moonlight round he had stumbled upon while out rearranging survey stakes.

That's the way it went for a while. The bartender brought another round and Yancey ordered bourbon and water. It was not the kind of place that had a jukebox but there was music coming from somewhere behind the bar. Chip chattered with Susan while Yancey endured the others until he could stand it no more. Chip slipped behind the bar and fiddled with some wires and, grinning, eased back in around the table. The speakers popped and buzzed and spit out some crackling blues. Not the Delta blues, not the Chicago blues, but crackling Muzak blues, white-man style with the bottom bleached out.

"Sorry, honey," Chip said to Susan as she resumed stroking his thigh. "That's the best we got in this joint."

At least it was the blues and if you listened hard enough you might hear a ghost of a dirty back beat. Miss Cassie stood and jiggled. She had a nice ass and her belly had a slight pucker like a gal in those old Italian paintings.

Miss Cassie clapped her hands. "'M'on, boy," she said with open arms to Yancey and faking a kiss. "Dance with me."

Yancey hesitated, glanced at Susan.

"No, honey," Miss Cassie said, "you can dance with her later. You dance with me now."

"Dance with Johnny," Chip piped in.

"I think he's married," Yancey said.

Chip raised his martini and an eyebrow. "Honey, they're all married … 'cept me."

Chip minced and Susan smirked and Miss Cassie shook her tail like a duck leaving water.

The things Miss Cassie did to Yancey on that floor. She was a knee-knocker. She moved her hands one way, her feet another, her fanny the other, and she bent forward and backed up and bumped Yancey's crotch with her ass. She rubbed her breasts along his arms, arched her back and humped his leg, howled like a porno queen. Susan loved it. Chip stood and applauded, then joined them on the floor, hovering like a disco duck around Yancey's leg.

This went on for an hour or so and when they staggered out and sat on the front steps a little after eleven they eyed each other, wondering who would sleep with whom, like drunks usually do. Yancey never got the chance to dance with Susan or to talk to her much. Miss Cassie was always in the way, once slipping off her sandals and running her toes around his ankles and giving him a lap dance, at which point Yancey excused himself saying he had to take a leak. When he returned fifteen minutes later, she was too drunk to finish what she had started.

They sat talking on the front steps and sipped their drinks from plastic to-go cups. The gators grumbled out in the swamp and the mockingbirds yodeled up the moon and Henrietta Ford, tied out front to a porch post, broke wind.

Yancey recalled another Bible story about Balaam's talking ass. The King of Moab sent his prophet Balaam over to curse the Children of Israel, but the Lord dispatched an angel to block the way. Balaam could not see the angel but the ass could, and balked. When Balaam whipped his mount, the ass turned around and said in perfect King James English, "Why dost thou beat me? Have I ever failed thee?"

It was the second time in the Good Book that an animal spoke. The first was when the snake propositioned Eve in the Garden. Old Balaam might have known the snake story, maybe not, but a talking ass was inspiring. Instead of cursing the Children, he blessed them.

In the Age of Miracles, Henrietta would have busted loose in Gullah if she could talk, aggrieved not by the lash but by being ridden across the island bareback, through the security gate and tethered to a porch post in the dark. But the Age of Miracles had come and gone, so Henrietta simply broke wind.

"What the hell was that?" Johnny asked.

"Oh, Johnny," Chip gushed, "I didn't know you cared."

Susan Drake laughed and told Chip that Johnny was already taken. When Henrietta stomped a hoof against the pavement, Susan looked at Yancey and said, "Tell me you didn't ride a horse here tonight."

"No ma'am," Yancey said. "Didn't ride a horse."

"A stud," Chip giggled. "The man's a stud."

Susan breezed around the corner of the piazza and came back lit up like the moonrise, still more than an hour away. "Give me a ride."

Yancey untied Henrietta, slung himself onto the mule's back and hauled Susan up behind him.

They left the others there to ponder further permutations. Susan held tight to Yancey's waist. He could smell jasmine perfume again, along with girl sweat mixed with mule sweat. "How you doin'?" he asked.

"I can hardly breathe."

Yancey gave the mule his heels. Henrietta tossed her head back and cocked her ears and the three of them bounded off into the night, leaving a steaming pile of manure upon the inn's flagstone walk, bricks from the chimney of the big house, also long gone.

# SIXTEEN

Yancey took the bit from Henrietta's mouth and turned her loose at Susan's back door. The mule took a tentative step, then looked at Yancey as if to say, "You done set me loose now, boss, so goodbye." Henrietta broke into a trot and then a canter and thundered off into the darkness.

"Your ride just left you," Susan said.

"I'll get another."

She was halfway up the front steps. The lights were on inside and the front door was open. "Want a drink?"

The porch was awash in jasmine – climbing posts, pickets and rails, past its prime but still blooming.

"I'd have given ten bucks to see Henrietta clear the gate," he said.

Susan laughed. "They logged in one man on muleback; they'll log out one mule. Think they'll come looking for the man?"

"No ma'am," Yancey said.

"You ride mules often?"

"No ma'am." Yancey plunged his face into a mass of jasmine vine and the aroma filled his soul. He followed her inside.

Susan Drake's bar was better stocked than the one at the clubhouse. She had two kinds of single-malt scotch, which Yancey would not drink because Yankees did. There were three or four brands of vodka and some gin bottles with a variety of labels, along with obscure rums – brown, gold and black as molasses. There were sour mash whiskies of various persuasion; some of the bottles were numbered. She had an array of bar accessories – strainers, shakers, stirrers and such – and bottles of seltzer, spritzer and tonic, with and without citrus. The equipment was dusty, the bottles were not.

"Got any Red Stripe?" he asked.

The house had ten-foot ceilings with fans for hot summer afternoons and walls paneled in white. Large doors opened to a screen porch. The seven-foot-long marlin hung on the wall behind the bar.

"You catch that?" Yancey asked.

"Yes. Fought it for three hours. They poured sea water on me and I cried."

"Where?"

"Cabo."

"Where?"

She had no beer so Yancey chose whisky instead – sour mash mixed strong in a tall plastic tumbler with *Daufuskie Island Club and Resort* printed on the side. He turned it so he could not read the words and leaned against the kitchen counter and watched her mix a vodka and orange.

"Fish much?" he asked.

"I try and go once a year."

"Once a year? I'll take you sometime. We'll get after some sea trout."

Streaks of mule sweat circled the inside of her thighs, lather-lines like those left on motel linens washed in cheap detergent. Susan stirred her drink with her middle finger, and she wobbled as she walked – but not toward him. She stumbled onto the porch. Yancey saw her face light up briefly as she fired a cigarette, and he thought, *When I come to remember this gal, I want to remember her like she is right now.*

The cigarette coal bobbed in the dark like a Clark spoon lure in phosphorescent water. Yancey topped off his drink and joined her. The eastern sky was illuminated and the stars were beginning to fade. Orion, the mighty hunter, to the southeast, stood upside down this time of year.

"Moon will be up directly," he said.

Susan sat on a large porch swing that hung from chains heavy enough to yank trucks out of a mud bog. The swing was as big as a single bed and layered three feet deep with overstuffed pillows. She patted the one beside her left thigh. "Come, watch for the moon with me."

Yancey sat down in the swing, took a long drink and placed the tumbler on an end table to free both hands. She put her head on his shoulder and looked up at him with those blue neon eyes.

"Why did you come tonight?" she asked.

"You asked me," he said as he wrapped his right arm around her shoulder and sighed.

"Yes, but what do you expect from me?"

Deep in the woods, an owl hooted and a bull gator grumbled and a host of bullfrogs croaked in baritone. "Well, I didn't expect you to run a parade of queers by me."

She stiffened, peeled his hand from her shoulder like it was the putrid remains of road-kill possum. "Mr. Yarboro, I don't appreciate your talking about my friends like that. They are people, just like us."

Yancey grabbed his tumbler and threw back a slug. "They might be your friends and they might be people, but that don't mean I gotta like 'em."

She cut her eyes his way. "Knowing what little I know about you, I imagine you'd think people have the right to be themselves."

"Got to agree with that," Yancey said, "so long as they can take an ass-kicking."

The neon flashed like fire. "And you? Ever get your ass kicked for being who you are?"

"Ma'am," he said, "you don't even know."

She sighed and settled her head back into the pillows. "Guess not. How long did you say you been living here?"

"I didn't," he said.

"How long?"

"Off and on my whole life."

"Ever been to New York City?"

"No ma'am."

"Chicago?"

"No ma'am."

"Think maybe you've missed anything?"

"Only what I didn't mind missing much."

"Why do you keep calling me ma'am?"

"Respect," Yancey said.

Her head was back on his shoulder by then. "Really?"

"Yes ma'am."

"There you go again."

"Yes ma'am."

Yancey had run ma'aming her about down to nothing. So he looked at her and she looked at him and there wasn't much left to do but start kissing.

He leaned to her and she leaned to him, and the thunder of his pulse rose in his ears. Their lips touched. Susan turned her head sideways and parted her lips and their tongues met and their souls leapt.

"You smell like jasmine," she said as she caught her breath.

"Yes ma'am," he said. "You do, too."

He pulled her to him with his right hand and held her chin with his left while their tongues played tag. She grabbed the front of his shirt and pulled him closer. The buttons popped off. *Who in the hell am I gonna get to sew them back on?* he wondered.

But he didn't think about it long because they rolled out of the swing and onto the floor and they were on their knees facing each other and he removed her top, careful not to tear off any of her buttons. Her breasts were round and full. Her nipples were hard, so he started nibbling, and fire rose up within her. He pulled off her shorts and she helped, but when he got to her silk thong panties she said, "Wait. No!"

Yancey's jeans were down around his knees now and his left pocket was convenient to his left hand, so he reached down and grabbed his knife, a big folding skinner sharp enough to shave with.

He snicked it open and Susan looked at it the way a rabbit eyes a coiled snake. He put the palm of his hand in the middle of her breastbone, pressed her back flat on the floor, and he didn't have to push very hard. His eyes never left hers. He heard himself thinking, *Damn, here I am drunk and fixing to cut somebody. I must be spending too much time with the Mexicans.*

But like most things Yancey thought, it wasn't for long. When he reached for the spot at the point of her hip where the sheer black silk was narrowest, his eyes left hers and she tried again to stop him.

Too late. *Snip* – her panties fluttered like a dying bird onto the front porch floor.

She lay naked, helpless and bleeding. That's when Yancey realized he had sliced her forefinger in the process, opened it from knuckle to nail. She smiled, held it up for him to see. Now he was the rabbit and she was the snake. The blood ran down her arm onto her belly, pooled in her navel, then dripped to the floor.

She held her bleeding finger to his mouth and he sucked it like a vampire. And the curious old moon peeked over the edge of the world, lighting up a pewter pathway across the sea in all of God's glory.

And little waves not far away said, *Yes, yes, yes!*

SEVENTEEN

"Watch out fuh dem Baptist," Gator Brown warned. "They eat yo' chicken and spote yo' wife."

"Mink and coon ate all my chicken," Yancey countered, "and ain't got no wife."

"Man like you could use one."

"One chicken ain't no good," Yancey said. "Won't lay no eggs and die of lonesome."

"You die of lonesome, too," Gator Brown said, paused and looked out his front window at the pecan tree loaded with green nuts. Gator Brown's relic of a .22 rifle leaned on the wall behind the door. It was a '58 Chevy bumper-jack kind of a gun – rusty and beat up, but it always fired. Gator Brown watched for squirrels. Squirrel meat is sweet, and boiled up with onions and celery makes better stew than chicken despite so many little bones.

Yancey had a lump in his throat and a pain in his heart as he sat there with Gator Brown. Susan Drake was back to Atlanta and left him choked up inside. He figured he'd better do something quick. Yancey went to church occasionally – funerals and baptisms mostly. It was a lot of trouble to get there all hung over as he generally was on Sunday mornings. But he always left church feeling better than when he arrived. He needed to feel better that morning, so he left the tractor with his Mexicans and struck out on foot for the eleven-fifteen service. It was ten-thirty when he reached Gator Brown's place. He'd been carrying Susan Drake's panties around in his back pocket ever since the night he cut them off. He took them out from time to time and nosed them when nobody was looking. Now he took them out of his back pocket and passed them across the table.

Gator Brown whistled. "Now you is talkin' chick'n!"

"You help me, Gator Brown?"

Gator Brown looked down at the panties, then up at Yancey. "Dem real nice. How dey get cut like dat?"

Yancey changed the subject. "How 'bout that tax man?"

"What tax man?"

"The one you was workin' on the other night."

"Oh him? Too early yet to know. Watch, though. Sump'in always happen."

"What'll it cost me?" Yancey asked.

Gator Brown shook his head, held up the palm of his hand like a school crossing guard does to halt traffic. "Be careful, boy. Don' come round six month f'um now tellin' me you ain' want it no mo'."

"She ain't like the other ones," Yancey said.

"Better hope not. Who dat last gal you brung over?"

"Which one?"

"You knows which one."

Yancey thought about Tara Lynn, and it pained him. "Don't matter no more. How much you charge?" Yancey asked again, only he was speaking Gullah and said *chaahge*.

"Mr. Yance, you always been good to ol' Gator Brown. I give you de fambly discount."

"How much?"

"Five hun'red dollah."

"Great God, man! You bad as the swindlin' lawyer!"

"What lawyer dat is, Mr. Yance?"

Yancey did not want to tell him about Wilton K. Ramsey, Esquire, and the five thousand dollar retainer the lawyer had demanded for his services; about what it might cost all said and done to have the Judge declared incompetent; about what it might cost to own his own ground; about how he could hardly do that even if he had the money; about how he might have to anyway.

"Well, he is incompetent, ain't he?" lawyer Ramsey had asked Yancey about the Judge, and Yancey had shrugged and said, "I reckon."

Folks laughed about it all the time, over coffee at the Ocean View Cafe or over whisky at the Yacht Club. But snickering over drinks and testifying in a court of law are different matters, and even if Yancey could get witnesses and even a doctor or two, there was still his mother. She might sell the land herself, even if the Judge could not. When it was all over, the lawyers might get more than the land was worth to start with.

But Yancey figured Gator Brown knew all this anyway since Gator Brown knew damn near everything, so there was no need to talk about it.

"Grabe-yaad walkin' be hard on ol' Gator Brown."

"Why you go to the graveyard?"

"Why, Mr. Yance, gots to get goofer dust to do what you want me to. Dem spirit a-moanin' and carryin' on out dere, hangin' off tombstone and drippin' off tree limb and ting. Wear a man out jus' listen to 'em carryin' on. I sooner split ten cord of stovewood."

"Goofer dust?" Yancey asked.

"Yessir, Mr. Yance, dirt off a dead man grabe. Not jus' any dead man, neither."

"Which dead man you talkin' about, Gator Brown?"

"Jake Simmon," Gator Brown said. "You know ol' Jake?"

Yancey remembered Jake. He sold moonshine and kept loaded dice in his back pocket to fleece the shrimpers and the barge deckhands. Once he got caught in the tool shed with Miss Evangeline, her dress thrown up over her hips, her underwear jerked down around her knees and ol' Jake getting after her like a billy goat.

"Jake ghost come shrew de woods like a ball of fire," Gator Brown said, as if he'd seen it many times. "You gots to get dat goofer dust at dead-time, Mr. Yance, and dat be midnight. You gots to feed 'um wid match head and gunpowder and ..."

"I'll go get the dirt off ol' Jake's grave," Yancey interrupted. "For five hundred dollars, I'll get a bushel basket full. I'll get it at midnight for no extra charge and you can feed it whatever you want."

That brought Gator Brown up short. "Huh?" he said. "You brang 'um to me?"

"Yeah," Yancey said. "Graveyard don't fret me none."

"Ought to."

"Well, it don't."

"You sho'?"

"Sho', I sho'."

"Huh," Gator Brown said again as he scratched his head. "Grabe ya'd ain' worry you, boy? You must be fool. Lode Jesus say you got days, you got hair on yo' head, but you can't count neither one."

"I ain't countin'," Yancey said.

Gator Brown considered this for a moment and shook his head with great sadness. "Don't take no bushel basket, jus' a spoon'll do. Maybe I can do 'um a l'il cheaper."

"How much cheaper?"

"You got a hundred dollah?"

Yancey had only a wrinkled twenty in his pocket for the collection plate at First African Baptist, and this was not one of those churches where they passed it around. No sir. They left it up front and the whole blessed congregation would get up and file past and throw cash money in, and the preacher and the deacon would give the evil eye to anybody who just sat there.

So Yancey skipped church that day. He hauled the twenty out of his pocket and passed it to Gator Brown. "This all I got now. My credit any good?"

Gator Brown licked the bill and held it up to the light. "You knows you alway got credik wid ol' Gator."

"I'll pay you the rest when I bring the dirt."

Gator Brown, still savoring the twenty, said. "Look here, Mr. Yance, all this comercializin' done got me thirsty. I buy you a drink?"

"Gator Brown, you know there ain't no bar open on Sunday 'round here."

Gator Brown eased up to his feet. "Come on, Mr. Yance, we fetch up Henrietta Fode and go to the Beach Club."

Well, this is something, Yancey thought. The Beach Club was just down from the inn and they did not take money there, just membership cards. Yancey followed him out the door. "You got a still somewheres?"

Gator Brown laughed, "How you talk, boy. Ain' fired no still in forty-odd year."

When Henrietta Ford saw Yancey, she rolled her eyes and laid back her ears and shifted her hind legs like she was going to kick him into next Tuesday. But Yancey stood clear and she settled down when

Gator Brown brought out the harness. By the time he backed her into the traces, she was her old self again. Gator Brown fetched up a shovel and a long piece of iron rod and threw them into the wagon box. They climbed aboard and Gator Brown clucked at the mule and they creaked and rolled down the sandy track toward the sea.

They passed through the Daufuskie Island Club and Resort front gate, where the barrel-bellied guard stood in the road lest they try any more nonsense with their mule-drawn conveyance. They passed the First African Baptist Church where the black-suited elders perched along the porch rail like crows on a fence wire. They passed the faithful headed up the road to church in beat-up pickups and tattered sedans while Yancey and Gator Brown went the other way.

They went on down past the Dueling Oak, where the hot-blooded aristocrats used to come from miles around to settle their differences, chivalrous-like, with pistols and blades. And they passed a string of derelict shanties, forlorn ever since their owners had gone to find work in Savannah. They passed Yancey's Mexicans in a truck hauling a load of tomatoes to the landing and he gave them the high sign, but they crossed themselves and looked away when they saw Gator Brown driving the rig.

And at last they reached the beach. Gator Brown tied Henrietta to a driftwood snag and gathered up the tools and they walked south along the dune line far enough for Yancey to wish he had gone to church instead. Then Gator Brown pointed to a swale behind a dune and said, "Right chere."

Gator Brown jabbed the rod in the ground and probed around real careful, working the iron gently into the loose sand – one, two feet deep. It was like when Yancey was a boy and he checked sea turtle nests using an oak stick, probing for egg white stuck on the end of the wood. You could cook a turtle egg till Jesus came back and the white would always be runny. Old women liked them for baking 'cause turtle-egg cakes always stayed moist. You could sell the eggs for two bucks a dozen back then.

Yancey heard a faint clink when the rod hit some glass. Gator Brown grinned so wide Yancey thought his face would bust in two. "Dig," Gator Brown said, "but dig easy."

Yancey worked real slow with the shovel, then pushed away the last layer of sand with his hands and found the bottle. It was brown glass with a weathered cork and no label. Yancey picked up the bottle and shook it and it was full. He passed it to Gator Brown.

"How'd this get here?" Yancey asked.

"Dey chunk 'em ober-bode back when I jes' a chile 'cause de rebel-nooer come round."

"Who chunked 'em," Yancey asked. "Rum-runners?"

"Yessir, but dis ain' rum..."

Gator Brown brushed the sand from the bottleneck, worked loose the cork. He tipped it up and took a long pull, wiped his lips with the back of his hand and passed the bottle to Yancey. "Dis be Biblical," Gator Brown smacked. "Thy rod and thy spade dey comfut me."

"That would be *staff*, Gator."

"No, Mr. Yance, dat ain' make no sense. A rod and a staff 'bout de same ting. How a man gonna dig up whisky wid-out no shovel?"

Yancey took the bottle. "Dig? They weren't diggin', they was runnin' sheep."

Gator Brown shook his head. "Sheep? Mr. Yance, you daddy hab 'em at one time, and you knows dey ain' no comfut in sheep! Somebody muss up de translate."

Yancey tried to explain to Gator Brown it was the sheep that were comforted, not the shepherd, but Gator Brown wouldn't hear of it. "Nossir, dey be diggin' up likka, for tru't. You know dey talks 'bout de Bomb in Gilead? Well, dat what dis be."

Yancey took a drink and it was Yankee scotch, but not the kind he had tried once before. Not the scotch that makes you want to shake your head till your jowls flap and your teeth rattle. This was the smoothest whisky he had ever tasted, went down like liquid gold.

He passed the bottle back to Gator Brown, who took another long pull, then rocked on his heels and wiggled his toes. "Yessir, Mr. Yance, life jus' too shote for cheap likka and tight shoe."

EIGHTEEN

White folks don't mess round with conjuring much. For Gullahs, it's the last option in matters of money, luck, law and love. It's where to go when their ain't no place left to turn. Yancey was among the Gullahs now. Seldom had he been away from them in his entire life. Heartsick and lonesome, he was down to his last option.

Yancey had studied the moon, especially because it bothered him so, what with the copper sliver stuck in his head and all. He knew the phases of the moon, and all the risings and the settings thereof: How the moon goes around the earth in twenty-seven days, seven hours and forty-three minutes, and how the sun illuminates the half of the moon facing it, except during lunar eclipses, when the moon passes through the earth's shadow, and he had seen only one of those. The moon is full when the sun and moon are on opposite sides of the earth – that's when it shines like a mirror in the dark. When the moon is between the earth and the sun, it reflects no light, and that's what's called a new moon. In between, the moon's illuminated surface waxes full, then wanes down to nothing, until it's new again.

They call the edge of the moon shadow "the Terminator." It's almost always curved, concave to the half moon; it looks like somebody lopped off an orange with a machete. It's convex when it gets close to full. Because the horns of the moon at the ends of the crescent always face away from the setting or rising sun, they point upward in the sky. It annoyed Yancey greatly whenever he saw paintings with the horns pointing downward.

He memorized a poem in high school about the crescent moon with a star between its tips. He decided it's not a star at all, but Venus in midwinter, rising just before the sun. Or maybe Mars or Jupiter. It's as bright and intense as old Yaweh's burning rage. If you have a good pair of binoculars, you can see that whatever it is has phases, too. Star or planet, it can't shine through the moon, unless the moon had a hole in it, which it doesn't. But Yancey's heart had a hole in it now.

Damn-it all to hell, he thought. He had been perfectly happy the way things were, sporting Tara Lynn or somebody like her, knocking off a hot little stray now and then. But he didn't give a damn for the others now.

It was a lie, of course. He was not perfectly happy – never had been – but he got by. Now he was in love and he begrudged the misery that came with it. He did not know misery was another part of being in love. So he figured he'd try being furious for a bit, which was easier than moping around like his dog just died.

Yancey didn't have a dog, but he was planning to get one when things settled down. Maybe he'd get a Chesapeake bitch, curly haired, yellow-green eyes and a good nose. He'd buy her young and keep her with him always. He would train her to fetch ducks and to paw in the cooler and bring him a beer. She'd sleep on the doormat on the front porch and she'd chew the ass off of anybody skulking round out there after dark.

He got the tractor back from his Mexicans and the crew chief, Ramon Fernandez, looked at him sideways like he knew he was up to something.

"*Quién es tu mujer?*"

Yancey responded in the best Spanish he could muster, "*No tengo mujer.*"

Ramon Fernandez shook his head and his eyes danced in the firelight. He mumbled something Yancey did not catch. They had another tomato picking on the last field and they soon would be gone. And there'd be a new crew next year, men who wouldn't know at first that they would be working on an island with *muchos mosquito y ningún cantina.*

Yancey always shot a deer just before they left. He considered it a kind of tip, so they might come back. They always roasted it on hickory wood, sucked venison from its bones while singing their mournful Mexican songs. They never came back.

Now, as Yancey's Ford tractor clattered down the road, running with the one headlight that still worked, he could see their campfires flickering through the trees.

Lighthouse Road pretty much split the island north and south, from the old government dock on Calibogue Sound to the ruins of the beacon tower which guided sailing ships into Savannah in the old days. Seaward of the road were old cotton fields, grown up now with live oaks and yellow pines, most of them older than everybody's great-great-granddaddy. These woods were dark and dreary and wonderful. All were thick now except one, Daufuskie Island Plantation, now Daufuskie Island Club and Resort, with the gate and guards and all. Landward was ground given to the slaves, and lights shone dimly through the windows of some of the shanties still standing. Only twenty-six descendants remained.

The government paved the road in the '40s when a Coast Guard contingent was stationed on Daufuskie – the Pony Patrol, they called themselves, riding horses up and down the beach, looking for German saboteurs slipping ashore from submarines. The Germans never showed up, so the Coast Guardsmen marked time currying their horses, squinting out to sea, sampling the local 'shine and brown girls. When the war ended they went home, leaving a road and some babies the color of Moo-Cow caramel candy. The babies grew up and left the island too, like just about everybody else, and the road became potholed and weeds grew in the cracks. The half-mile from the Daufuskie Island Club and Resort front gate to the ferry landing bore a thin coat of blacktop that everybody knew wouldn't last long.

Yancey drove past the derelict lighthouse and the cottage where the keeper used to live. The woods had overtaken the grounds, and here and there between the young pines and scrub oaks were great ornamental shrubs from previous days: azaleas, camellias and oleanders. Fruit trees, too, and if you got there before the Gullahs stripped them to fill demijohns of homemade wine, you could eat plums and pears and – in good years – all the oranges at Christmas your belly could hold.

Past all this, Yancey drove his tractor, then he turned onto a sandy lane covered in wax myrtle and cassina – a tunnel of green in the single headlight, branches clawing at him as he passed. He drove until he could drive no more, parked his tractor and walked down a trail you couldn't find unless you knew where it was.

The slaves buried their dead on the back side of the island, near creeks and rivers, the graves facing east so the spirits could fly back to Africa on the Great Gettin'-Up Mornin' that was sure to come some day. In Africa, a funeral might last a week, and mourners would arrive from miles around to satiate the demons of death with food, drink, dance, song and sex. But the slave masters wanted none of that. Each plantation had its own burying ground so the slaves wouldn't waste time walking all over the island to attend funerals.

After freedom, the Gullah wanted to be planted among their kin when their time came. So the cemeteries slowly grew inland from ranks of oblong depressions along the river, from where there used to be cypress boards sticking up instead of stone markers. Next came a few homemade ones, concrete poured into wooden forms, names and dates scratched into the drying slurry with a nail.

There were two rashers of government stones – one for veterans of the First World War, one for the Second – with the names of the dead and the numbers of Negro regiments carved into the markers. Not far away stood a single store-bought stone etched with the image of hands folded in prayer and the name "Jake Simmons" under which was written, "Leaning on the Everlasting Arms."

Yancey could not read what it said in the moonlight, but he had seen it hunting deer years before. He knew that Jake Simmons liked to lean on trees, shovels, porch posts, tool sheds and outhouses when he was dead drunk, but he never leaned on Jesus until he was on his deathbed, which Yancey reckoned the Lord bore with considerable skepticism. But that did not matter now. Jake was gone to goofer dust, and Yancey, down to his last option, was there to get some.

The moon ghosted through the clouds like great lumps of silver with the edges polished bright. Yancey picked his way through the graveyard with the best flashlight he had, which wasn't much. He knelt beside the stone and checked his watch – a quarter to midnight – and he prayed "Jake, you old bastard, don't you let me down."

Yancey raked the leaves away, found some soft damp earth, scooped a fistful and dumped it into a Ziploc bag he had pulled from his pocket.

His momma told him a story about her college days, how they sent a sorority pledge into a graveyard at midnight and told her to drive a stake into the center of a grave to prove she had been there. The girl picked up a large rock, knelt down and drove the stake through the hem of her skirt, and when she tried to stand back up, she thought the Death Angel had hold of her. They found her body there the next morning, face down upon the grave, dead as a mackerel. Yancey trembled as he placed seven new dimes upon the grave like Gator Brown told him to do. The flashlight was just strong enough for him to make sure they were all heads up.

Yancey stood, rolled up the plastic bag, squeezed out the air and shoved it into the pocket of his jeans. He stepped back and, sure enough, the Death Angel grabbed hold of him, too. Backward he went, tripping over something big, knocking his head on a nearby stone, sprawled into a tangle of devil vine, which is as wiry and stickery a plant as you will find in these parts.

"What the hell!" he hollered. *"Jesus H. Christ!"*

He struggled to his knees and groped for his flashlight but could not find it. Instead he felt a rough burlap bag, then another and then more, stacked around him like a host of spirits having a confab in the dark.

He recognized the smell. He fumbled for his skinning knife, the same one that had drawn blood from Susan Drake, sliced into one of the bags, pulled out a bud and held it up in the moonlight. It was the size of a duck egg, and as gummy as Georgia pine resin.

Later, after he got the stuff home and padlocked safely in his shed, he delivered the goofer dust to Gator Brown. Yancey looked the old man square in the eyes and said, "Gator Brown, what exactly did you send me out there to find?"

Gator Brown grinned and said, "I just sent you, Mr. Yance, and you found what you need."

But all of that came later. Right now he was on his knees in a slave graveyard at midnight, the history and magic and grief upon him like a whirlwind, a dead man's dust in his pocket and four hundred and forty pounds of marijuana lying in a great tangle of devil vine.

NINETEEN

Yancey felt her foot as she slept beneath the covers. Her heel was rough going one way, and smooth the other, like sharkskin. He ran his fingers along her high arch, and at the ball of her foot he found the same kind of skin again. The bones of her ankle were delicate and the swell of her calf firm, her skin softer the higher he went. Her inner thigh felt like a calf's nose, but not wet, yet.

She came back to the island six months later. He had just about given up watching the ferries, given up scanning the faces on the upper deck where he knew she would ride in late summer. Time and again he polished the haze from his dented binoculars in search of a tall yellow-haired woman. He saw many but not one was her.

It was way down in August now and the tomatoes were gone to market. He was harrowing his fields, and the creeks were full of mullet and a hurricane churned somewhere out there between Daufuskie and Africa. He had almost given up this ritual when he saw her on the ferryboat the day the cell phones quit working.

Cell phones never work well on Daufuskie, too far away from the ugly relay towers alongside Interstate 95. Even when they did work you couldn't hear them over the clatter of the ferry diesels. It amused him to see the golfers snap open their clamshells the minute they were clear of the diesel racket, as if they expected a monumental deal had closed during the forty-five-minute boat ride.

Yancey was often half-drunk, hanging off his porch railing watching those men in knit shirts and khaki pants and two-toned shoes. *Smash it, smash it,* he'd say to himself about their cell phones. *Lay it on the dock and let the baggage cart crush it. Throw the sumbitch overboard.*

But this time the cell phones did not work at all. Maybe a semi ran off the interstate and clipped a tower. Maybe Gator Brown put the root on 'em. Yancey did not know and he did not care.

Not long ago, he was down at the county dock on the south end of the island when a Savannah tour boat was loading up day-trippers for the ride back. A seepy shrimp boat was tied alongside some skiffs and the tour boat was jammed in between. When the mate scurried forward to fend off the bow of the tour boat from the shrimp boat's stern, the mate's cell phone fell from his top pocket into the water.

Yancey saw all this and applauded, and a dozen or so locals standing along the bank clapped too. When the mate grinned at the crowd and held his thumbs up, Yancey figured there was still some hope for mankind.

But this day nobody dropped any phones overboard. Up to the dock they trekked, a dozen or so tourists with phones to their ears, shaking their heads, fumbling with the redial buttons. Susan Drake breezed along among them, walking with an easy grace as if she'd been gone only a little while. Yancey's heart pounded.

He wanted to shout, run to her, bog the hundred yards of pluff mud and marsh that separated them, fall at her feet, clasp her around the knees and bury his face in her dress like he did with his momma before he got too old for such things and whisky turned his momma sour.

But he did not. He figured she would take the resort bus to her place, wait for the bellmen to bring her groceries to the house, maybe even put the groceries away for her. She'd pour herself a vodka and orange and wait for the sun to go down. She'd come to him after dark.

He was mostly right. The screen door to his cabin creaked open and swooshed shut, but it was still broad daylight. She stood at the threshold and slowly unbuttoned her dress, letting it drop to her feet, and she looked at him with the saddest eyes he had ever seen.

They made love that day – twisting, wheeling, clawing at each other like ospreys mating on the wing. Afterward she returned from the bathroom wearing his only dress shirt and said, "I'm bleeding."

"Did I hurt you?"

"No. What makes you think you could?"

He knew women were damn near bulletproof down there, that even old King Solomon – who had nine hundred some-odd wives plus God only knows how many concubines, supposedly the wisest man in the Bible – was the dumbest sumbitch who ever lived.

"Did any of your other ... lady friends leave tampons?" she asked.

There were some in the cabinet under the sink and they'd been there for a while. A couple of weeks before, Yancey had run out of rolling papers so he used a tampon wrapper to twist joints from the reefer out in the shed. "I think I have some somewhere," he said.

He brought them to her. She went back into the bathroom, then returned to the bed. "I don't know what's wrong with me," she said. "I haven't had a period in years."

Her head was on the pillow and Yancey propped himself up on one elbow at her side.

"You have company when I was gone?" she asked.

"A dozen Mexicans."

"No *senoritas?*"

"No ma'am."

"There you go again."

"Yes ma'am. And you?"

She turned away. "No girls," she said.

"I didn't mean that."

"I do have a husband, you know."

"I know."

They stared at each other as the sun slipped down toward Savannah and the August marsh was the color of ripening wheat. The tide was in full flood and Yancey could feel it vibrating like an anchor line taut in the current. Out back in the pines, a whippoorwill called for a mate that refused to come, and Yancey knew how that bird felt.

"What all you been up to?" she asked.

"Getting my crop up. Lawyering."

"Lawyering?"

"Yeah. Trying to keep those swindling bastards from stealing my land."

A look rolled across her face like the shadow of a wind-driven cloud on a slick sea. "Stealing it? How could they steal it?"

"I worked it a dozen years, paid my rent 'cause I don't really own it."

Little drops of sweat lay like beads on her upper lip. She drew up her knees and grunted like a baby with the colic. "God," she said.

"What?" he asked.

"Cramps, Sweet Jesus."

"I got something for it," he said.

She raised an eyebrow. "Aren't you the perfect host? Tampons and Midol for all your girls."

This was her way, coming at him with something like this, because he had asked about her husband. She had kept to her side of the bed in the months she had been home, making typical excuses. Poogey Drake made a few feeble attempts but gave up, got what he needed elsewhere, as usual. But Yancey did not know this and she did not tell him.

"No ma'am. Ain't talking about Midol."

She stretched out again, waiting for the pain to subside, and when it did, she asked, "Wouldn't you be better off without that farm?"

"No ma'am."

"What's it worth?"

"Too good for golf," he said.

"I play golf," she said.

"I don't. Put a nine-iron in my casket and I'll haunt you forever."

"You could use the money."

"It's my daddy's ground."

"You could inherit it."

The sun cleared the trees now and light spilled over the distant pines, illuminating acres of marsh. The water and the sky and all creation were the color of scuppernong wine.

"A bad man lives forever," he said.

"What a thing to say! My father is the sweetest man in the world."

"Is he?"

She paused. "Yes."

"Mine ain't."

"Don't you love him?"

"Yes." He was about to add, *More than you can imagine.* But didn't.

"Why?"

"Why what?"

"Yancey Yarboro, you are a knot-head."

"Runs in the family."

He touched her left thigh but she pushed his hand away and drew up her knees again. "Ohhh," she moaned in pain.

"Let me get you something," he said.

"Lawyers cost money," she said. "Can you afford one?"

"Got a plan. Want something for those cramps?"

"Yes," she said feebly. "What is it?" Only it sounded like *Whatizit?*

He looked past her shoulder through the window to the river and he thought briefly that she might be right about him quitting the farm. He had felt that way the first time he saw her, when he was out rearranging survey stakes. *Give it all up*, he thought. *Give up that land. Give up everything. 'Cept her.*

But he would not lie down and sleep until the trumpet blew, like the preacher said it would after he was dead. He could quit the farm, scrape up some cash and buy a boat – a thirty-foot shrimper. Rework the engine. Install extra fuel and water tanks and a big grocery locker in the hold and they'd cruise to Bermuda, Barbados, beyond, forever. Pull off the winch and the booms and extend the cabin onto the rear deck.

The boat would look odd and they would name it *Whatizit*. He'd be happy then, in a world with no real estate sharpies and swindling lawyers. But would living on a boat make a woman like Susan Drake break out in hives?

"Reefer," he said. "I'll spin you up one. Make you feel better."

"I don't do drugs," she said.

"Never?"

"Well, Poogey really likes his coke."

"Cocaine will kill you," Yancey said. "Whatever's wrong with you, coke will make it worse. You'll think everything's fine till you fall flat and flop around on the deck like a mullet."

"Will reefer really help?" She wiped the sweat from between her breasts, held her hand up for him to see. He sucked her ring finger and tasted her pain, salty, slightly bitter, like the taste of a tarnished penny. "You're crazy," she said.

"Yes ma'am. How about it?"

"You smoke every day?"

"Only when I got it," he said.

"And you got it?"

"Yes, ma'am."

"OK," she said. "Can't make me feel much worse."

"It won't," Yancey said. "Guaran-damn-tee it."

He slipped on a T-shirt and a pair of cutoffs then eased across the back yard to his shed. She laid her head back on the pillow. It was nearly dark now and the scant shadows of his azaleas and camellias stretched along the ground. His flashlight had not worked since that night in the graveyard. He fumbled with the lock on the shed door and, out of the shadows, a cold steel gun barrel pressed against the back of his neck.

"Make one move and I'll blow your freaking head off."

 # TWENTY

Yancey had it figured out. Four hundred pounds times a wholesale price of five hundred dollars was two hundred grand, and that would buy a lot of lawyering. He was not yet sure what kind of lawyering it would buy, but he knew the math, which left him an extra forty pounds to smoke until Jesus came back. But Jesus was slow coming and Christy Seabrook showed up first.

Dammit to hell! Yancey thought as he stood there with a gun barrel jammed into the back of his head.

Yancey slowly turned until the muzzle firmly circled the end of his nose. He had trouble seeing around it cross-eyed, but he determined that there were two men and the gun was a short-barreled pump like cops carry on the front seat of cruisers. The man with the gun was built like he toted concrete blocks for a living.

"I think you got something of ours," the other one explained. He was taller, thinner, better dressed. Both were tanned, like shrimpers, and talked like locals.

"Didn't see your name wrote on it," Yancey said.

"Unlock the freaking door," the gunman demanded and pressed the muzzle against Yancey's nose hard enough to draw blood.

Yancey's eyes watered. "Get that damn thing out of my face," he said. "Please?"

"Unlock the door," the gunman said again.

Yancey did not know much about Jimmy Hoffa, only that he was president of the Teamsters Union until he aggravated the wrong folks. They never found Hoffa's body, not even buried in the end zone of Meadowlands where everybody said it was. But he remembered one thing Jimmy Hoffa said: "Flee the knife; rush the gun."

It was not that guns were less dangerous than knives, but a man with a knife had to reach you in order to kill you, unless he could throw it real good, and there were damn few men who could do that right. But a twelve-gauge pump stuffed with double-ought shot could drop you at eighty yards, so it wouldn't do any good for Yancey to run. He'd been shot up in the war and had a couple of knives pulled on him that night at the Judge's place but right now he wasn't exactly sure what to do.

Yancey wished the Judge were standing over in the azalea bushes with his .38. But the Judge was laid up drunk about now, and Yancey was on his own. So, he decided he'd fumble the key and drop it and when the man with the gun leaned down to pick it up, he'd grab the barrel and wrap it around the sumbitch's head. The other man didn't appear to have a gun and Yancey figured he could punch him out. Now, if only Susan Drake didn't come half-naked out onto the porch and upset the proceedings ...

So Yancey palmed the key and dropped it. The gunman took two steps backward, pointed the gun at the center of Yancey's chest and said, "Pick it up."

So much for drama.

Yancey unlocked the shed door and swung it open and then the aroma hit them. "It all there?" the other man asked.

"Twenty bags," Yancey said, "minus what I done smoked."

"Call the boys with the boat," the second man said, then asked Yancey, "How much you done smoked?"

"Didn't weigh it, just smoked it."

The gunman kept his right hand at the wrist of the stock, his finger on the trigger. He reached into his pocket, grabbed a cell phone, pushed some buttons, held it to his ear. He shook his head, shook the phone, passed it to the other man and said, "It don't work."

Yancey decided right then that he kinda liked the guy.

The second man tried to get a dial tone, adjusted the little antenna and asked, "Cell phones work here?"

"Not lately," Yancey said.

"Who are you anyway?" he asked.

"Yarboro. Yancey Yarboro."

The men looked at each other and the gunman whistled. "The Judge's boy?"

"Yep," Yancey said, adding, "If I'da hid this reefer, you'da never found it."

"Hell," the second one said, "you hid it and we found it just fine."

"No, dammit, if I'da hid it in the first place ... And if I knew you'da come a-looking, you'da still be a-looking."

"What in hell were you thinking, we'd forget?"

"Didn't know what to expect. A man don't find four hundred pounds of reefer in a graveyard every day."

"A man don't lose four hundred pounds of reefer in a graveyard every day, either," the second one said. "What were you doing there anyway?"

"Look fellas, I'd feel a lot more sociable if that cannon wasn't in my face," Yancey said.

"Mike," the second one said.

So now Yancey had one name. Mike lowered the muzzle but kept his finger on the trigger. Yancey figured he could take Mike in half a second, but now he wondered if he really had too. "Pleased to meet you," Yancey said.

"Tell me about killing them burglars," Mike said.

"Never killed nobody."

"Well, they dead."

"My daddy did it. Don't you read the papers?"

"You had something to do with it."

"No, I was just there. Now that you know my name, I reckon I ought to know yours."

"You ain't in no position to be asking questions," the tall one said.

Yancey slowly pointed to Mike. "You're Mike," he said, "so I'm halfway there."

The other guy fiddled with his phone but it was hopeless. "I'm Christy. Can you run a boat?"

"Born in a boat," Yancey said.

"Need work?"

One way or another, Yancey decided, he was going to lose the reefer. But he might pick up a little cash, and keep his head, too.

"Can I say no?"

"Not really," Christy said.

Mike raised the gun again to Yancey's bumpy nose. "Don't make no difference to me."

"Well, how can I assist you gentlemen?" Yancey exhaled. His mother made an art form out of sarcasm. He wished she was over in the bushes with the Judge because she'd be proud of her only son 'bout now. *But then again, both these sumbitches would be dead 'bout now too,* Yancey thought.

"It seems we have lost communication," Christy explained, pointing to the phone. "We need to get back across the river."

Yancey was figuring how much to charge them for the ride when Christy said, "Mike, give him a grand."

"Do what?"

"I know what I'm doing," Christy said. "Give it to him."

"Hell, it's my money!"

"I'll pay you back."

"Last time it took you two weeks, Christy. This bastard stole our reefer and now you want me to pay him for it?"

"We're hiring him!"

Mike shook his head, hooked the shotgun in the crook of his arm, pulled out his wallet and peeled out ten hundred-dollar bills.

"Where's your boat?" Christy asked.

"Pulled up along the bank," Yancey said, pointing to the river.

"Grab a sack," Christy said.

"Damn!" Yancey said. "You didn't say nothing about heavy lifting!"

"You didn't ask," Christy said. "Get moving!"

"I got company," Yancey said.

"We know," Mike said. "You ought to get some shades."

So down to the river they went, each carrying a ten-kilo sack of weed, Mike keeping one hand free to hold the shotgun. Three times they passed by the bedroom window and three times he saw her there asleep on his bed waiting for him. But he was busy at the moment and his heart ached and his guts ached and the waxing moon jangled his brain.

And when they were on the other side of the river and the bags were stacked into the back of the pickup, Christy said, "We'll call you when the next load comes in. Might need more cash."

Yancey was glad to get shut of that pair, but never let on. "I don't expect you'll be sticking no more shotguns in my face."

Even in the dark, he could see Christy grinning. "Hey, it ain't loaded."

"Ain't loaded?" Yancey asked.

"We ain't out to hurt nobody, pal."

TWENTY ONE

"We sure scared the shit out of him," Mike laughed. "He 'bout crapped."

"Don't sell him short," Christy said. "Remember those burglars at his daddy's place."

They were in Mike's truck, a '62 Dodge panel delivery, rattling up U.S. 17 toward Charleston. They were up on the north side of the Combahee River, crossing sad old rice fields, some of them cleared with the sweat and blood of Mike's Irish ancestors, since by then slaves were too precious for wasting on pungo muck. The highway rose from the marshes to the high ground along the north bank. A scent of pine sweetened the road wind as they rolled through the cool green shade.

"Said he didn't have nothing to do with it," Mike said.

The Dodge ran hot if he pushed her much over fifty, so Mike kept an eye on the gauges.

"You can believe that if you want," Christy said.

The Dodge left the factory with only the driver's seat. It was the cheapest model – which was fine when it was used at the Parris Island Officers' Mess. Mike bought it at auction and even though they told him he had to paint over the red-and-yellow USMC and the crossed sabers on the doors, he never did.

Now he had a dog-gnawed recliner installed on the passenger side, tipped back with the footrest level with the dash. Christy was thus reposed, rolling a joint, taking in the scenery through his knees. They were smoking *shake* – powerful green dust that spilled from the bottom of the burlap sack Yancey had tapped.

"Think he won a couple of medals – a Purple Heart for sure, maybe a Bronze Star – the way he was riding that girl last night," Christy said.

Mike whistled. "We could have charged admission. A man would pay ten bucks to see that show."

"A woman, too," Christy said. "Ever heard girls at a male strip joint?"

"Nope, never did."

"Scream like cats in heat."

Mike and Christy were coming up fast behind a log truck at the Laurel Spring curve. It was a smoking diesel with battered fenders, long whippy pines poking out the back end, a greasy-looking Carolina swamp cracker at the wheel.

A Carolina swamp cracker has the Death Angel for a time keeper. He has fractured ribs, busted teeth, blown eardrums, and a patina of two-cycle oil and sawdust that won't come off without Strip-Eze. When a Carolina swamp cracker hits the road, he chug-a-lugs a six-pack of Bud, wraps his logs with a single chain and lets his Peterbuilt rip. Sometimes a log will joggle out, bounce on the blacktop and pinwheel into oncoming traffic. Other times the chain snaps and dumps the whole load on a station wagon full of tourists from New Jersey or somewhere. Either way, a swamp cracker rolling down South can kill you deader than a long-hauler strung out on Adderal having an intimate conversation with the chrome bulldog mounted on the hood.

Mike eased off the gas, dropped back a hundred feet, far enough to miss the flying bark and pine top off the swamp cracker's load. Christy ran his tongue along the Zig-Zag paper gum. "If we'd known who he was beforehand, you might'a wanted a shell in the gun."

Mike shook his head. "Never signed up to shoot nobody."

"If you try backing down a man like Yarboro, he'll kill you quicker than blue lightning."

The truck driver flipped on his right-turn signal and the blinker flashed feebly as he braked to turn onto a dirt road that ran down river to the sawmill. Mike pulled the panel truck around him, hit the gas and ran the old Dodge back up to fifty. "I reckon we got off lucky. We scared the shit out of him, got the pot and him to tote it, too."

"Yeah," Christy said. "Now he's working for us. We on a roll."

"Need a light?" Mike asked.

Like Poogey Drake, way off in Atlanta, Christy had too much money for his own good. He had slept late that morning and called Mike from the pay phone outside the Huddle House. "Gonna snow tonight up in Charleston," he said.

Mike did not have much money, but more now than he usually did. He figured he was about due for a nose full of good toot. Lord knows, he'd earned it.

"We'll take your truck," Christy said, "and travel *incog-Negro*."

Christy told him to pack light, so Mike stashed five hundred-dollar bills inside a slogging boot along with a fifty for incidentals.

Now they were on their way up to Charleston, over the brackish Combahee, then the blackwater Ashepoo, through Jacksonboro, Ravenel, Red Top and Avondale, and up over the wide Ashley River and down to the cobblestone streets of the Holy City.

Oh, Charleston! you sacred ground, where locals claim the Ashley and Cooper rivers meet to form the Atlantic Ocean. You conundrum, you cipher, you aging madam in the whorehouse of history. Beautiful and damned; burned, bombarded and earth-quaked, you nest of Rebels, you trumpeter of sedition, you great temple of culture and corruption.

Charlestonians may have fired on Fort Sumter and started the war over secession but they had no patent on the notion. New Englanders tried it first. European armies were busy massacring each other in the Napoleonic Wars and their navies were blockading each other's ports. American ships heading for England got stopped by the French; the Royal Navy stopped those heading for France. Finally, President Jefferson had enough, so he shut down American trade with all of Europe. New England ship captains, going broke, reasoned that, "By Providence, if we volunteered to sign up for this Federal Union, we ought to be able to sign out of it, too."

It was a compelling argument – expending a lot of newsprint, breath and commentary for ten years – but it never came to much. In the 1830s, Vice President John C. Calhoun of South Carolina took it up again, this time against tariffs and for expansion of slavery into the West. Charlestonians named a street in his honor.

Calhoun Street runs clear across the Charleston peninsula, from where sloops and schooners nudge floats in the Ashley River to the rumbling Eastside wharves along the Cooper. Halfway through is a big park with giant old oaks and a statue of Mr. Calhoun standing on a high marble pedestal looking south with his hand upraised as if to say, "You pigeons might get me way up here but you darkies never will."

Across from the park was a second-floor apartment overlooking an interior walled garden. There, according to Christy, a man was waiting with a pound of Colombian toot. Mike found a parking spot two blocks away and wrestled the Dodge into a space beside a tree-lined curb. Mike and Christy had walked about half a block when two men leapt from the bushes onto the sidewalk in front of them.

They looked like sewing machine salesmen, with guns. Mike thought he saw a flash of chrome that might have been a badge. But there was no mistaking the guns – two short-barreled revolvers. One man spun Christy around and shoved his face into a wall, jammed his pistol into the base of Christy's skull. The other man stuck his gun between Mike's eyes. One of the men was tall and had a harelip with a scar running up inside his nose. He didn't say much, just stood there pressing the gun deeper into the back of Christy's neck. The short one did the talking. He was half-a-man tall, two-men wide. Looked like he had been run though an industrial trash compactor. His belly lapped over his belt, his jowls over his collar; his face looked like an Olmec totem.

"You boys out shopping?" he asked.

Christy had a hard time talking with his face jammed up against the stucco wall, got pebbles in his mouth when he tried. "Justh goin' up the sthreet for a beer, offither."

The harelip had Christy's wallet out and fanned with one hand through the stacks of hundreds. "N'yeah?"

"That's one hell of a lot of beer," the short man said as he lifted Mike's wallet out of his back pocket.

"Evi-dence," the tall one said.

Mike and Christy eventually got their wallets back, minus the money.

"Whose old truck is that yonder?"

"Mine, sir," Mike said.

Christy got cuffed, hands behind and all clicked up until the metal bit his wrists.

The men marched them to the truck, a pistol now at the butt end of Mike's brain. The parade drew a few curious stares from passersby. Just business as usual in the Holy City.

Mike drove and Christy sat on the edge of the recliner, his hands cuffed still. The harelip crouched behind the driver's seat, the sight of his pistol tickling the hairs at the back of Mike's neck. The short man followed in a nondescript white Ford with solid black tires and silver-moon hubcaps.

"N'urn left," the harelip said.

Mike maneuvered through the stiffening afternoon traffic, feathering the clutch, easing the stick shift, dodging the potholes, a cocked .38 at the back of his head. The bag of reefer was under the seat.

Downtown Charleston disappeared in the rearview mirror as Rivers Avenue narrowed to two lanes. Traffic dwindled to nearly nothing. They crossed Wassamassaw Swamp, one of the few places on Earth spelled backward the same way it's spelled forward.

Christy was depressed. At any minute he expected an order to stop the truck, get out, kneel beside a soggy cypress stump and say his prayers. Just two more drug hits, the papers would say after the bodies were found.

Mike thought about gators, how they had no molars. They hauled fresh meat underwater and up into their dens, let it putrefy and soften before eating it. In a week, he reckoned, his and Christy's bones would be spread over forty acres of muddy bottom.

They passed a sign, a crude cross made of roofing tin. "Get Right," it said horizontally, "With God," down the middle. Vandals had taken a spray can and added "zilla" at the bottom.

"Drive," the harelip said.

TWENTY TWO

"You gonna open the door now, or do I gotta throw rocks until you do?"

Susan laughed, but her voice had a cold edge to it. "No rocks on this island."

"Well, conch shells then."

She was long gone from Yancey's place by the time he was through with Christy and Mike, but she left her mark on the crease of his sheet, menstrual blood darker than burgundy wine. He called her a dozen times and nobody answered. So he grabbed a jug of Heaven Hill, climbed onto the tractor and headed her way.

There was Heaven Hill and Old Heaven Hill, and both were good whisky even though they came in plastic bottles. Plain Heaven Hill was two bucks cheaper and Yancey called it Young Heaven Hill. You could pour either one into a decanter and serve it to somebody who didn't know and they'd smack their lips and say, "Damn, where'd you get this?"

Old or Young, it didn't matter. Each ran about half of what it should have been and neither bottle broke if the owner got drunk and dropped it in the rain.

It was not raining yet, but trying to. Yancey drove with one hand, held the bottle in the other. Thunder rattled his head and fire warmed his belly by the time he pulled into the woods, stopped a quarter-mile past the resort gate and jumped to the ground.

It was about *dayclean*, as the Gullah say. The east was streaking up and the whippoorwills had turned in and the warblers were twittering out in the cassina bushes and wax myrtles, emerald now in the fullness of the season.

Yancey hoofed it through the woods alongside a ditch dug by slaves, overgrown now with trees and the remains of trees and a hundred and fifty years of fallen leaves. He sucked on his bottle and imagined he heard Africans singing and swinging heavy grubbing hoes, a lilting song full of words he did not know.

Daufuskie is shaped like a shallow bowl, high at the north and south, high along the riverbank where he lived. Along the east, the dunes rose up a little and kept the storm water from draining into the sea. In the middle was a wonderment of gum and tupelo, soft maple and scattered cypress, water trees that stole the sky and left no bushes or grass beneath the canopy. The trunks were smooth, tall and straight, and where they belled at the stump he saw the gentle swells of women. Black water pooled here and wild irises bloomed there every spring. Even now, in late summer, water sluiced into his footprints. The land rose as he neared the sea and he could hear the surf working hard, mumbling up a storm.

The jasmine had peaked already, and the great green ballooning of it on Susan Drake's front porch lattice held only a few forlorn petals. It looked like tattered confetti along their parade route of love. Her door was locked, so he sat on the steps as the sun continued to rise and he drank Young Heaven Hill. After a while he fooled with the deadbolt but he couldn't slip it with his knife. He tried sticking his credit card between the lock brass and the frame, but that didn't work either.

He grabbed one of her straight-backed porch chairs and thought about throwing it through the window glass, then charging upstairs and into her room and taking her whether she wanted him or not. He reckoned down deep inside she'd love him for it, but he was too worn down to find out. By then he was drunker than he'd been in a long time, so he went back to the tractor and rode home and slept in his shoes, woke up, called her again and she answered the phone.

"Did you have to go all the way to Savannah to get what you were looking for?" she asked.

"No ma'am. I reckon I didn't have any reefer, after all."

A long silence.

"Yancey Yarboro," she finally said, "I don't know if I should believe a single word coming out of your mouth."

Yancey made a habit of telling the truth, even if it was a problem sometimes. "Call me what you want," he said, "but never call me a liar."

Another long silence.

Yancey figured if she would not speak, then he would. "You would not believe what happened."

"Try me."

"Can I see you?"

She sighed. "Drive to the lighthouse and walk north. I'll meet you on the beach in an hour."

He drove and she walked and when he got to the strand, he turned north like she told him, and he got off his tractor. There was the gentle curve of the shore, misted over with sea haze, salt-stunted oaks that looked like giant bonsai trees, sentinel pines and palmettos, hard-packed sand and a great glory of surf rolling up and sliding back. Storm clouds stacked up over the sea and the wind sang sad songs that suited a late August afternoon.

He had the beach to himself there between the throngs of Hilton Head and Savannah. His beach was always deserted. He saw bird tracks and deer tracks and turtle tracks and a single set of footprints with a narrow heel and a high arch. Whoever made them was stepping out in the other direction. He backtracked. *Damn, did I just fall out a stupid tree? Where is she?*

He turned and squinted south. Way down the beach he saw her coming his way, ghostlike, in the haze. But this time there was something swinging from her neck. He quickened his pace and when they were about a hundred yards apart, he saw it was a camera, a heavy old single lens reflex, now used only by art photographers.

She smiled, but did not laugh. And they could not embrace – too much camera in the way. They sat on a driftwood log, her on one end, him on the other. She would not look him in the eye. She looked at him through the lens instead.

She fooled around with shutter speed, aperture, focus. "Face out to sea," she said.

Yancey raised his chin, squinted toward the gray pencil-line where sky met water. "What am I supposed to be looking for?" he asked.

"Nothing. Just look."

Click, click, click, three quick exposures.

"Well, if I'm just looking," Yancey turned to face her, "I'd sooner be looking at you."

Click, click. "Just shut up and be beautiful."

"Beautiful? Maybe you're thinking of your other friends."

She was off the log now, on her knees in front of him. *Click, click.* "Yancey Yarboro, I am fixing to stick your face in the sand."

"Better bring a lunch," he said. "Gonna take you a while."

She sat on the log again, rewound the film and slipped the canister into her pocket. This one would not end up in the shoebox under the bed with all the others. She would haul it across the river to the photo lab. Yes, and she would take the others, too.

Still, she would not look him in the eye. She held her hands between her knees like a child and idly scribed an arc in the sand with her big toe, freshly painted ruby red. *"Whatizit,"* she said, "that makes me love you so?"

TWENTY THREE

While Yancey was learning even more about love, sixty miles to the north Christy and Mike were getting robbed. Christy, still handcuffed, and Mike, with a .38 at the back of his head, both thinking they were dead men.

They were in the truck in the swamp on a narrow concrete road and came upon one of those Stop and Robs – a combination gas station, motel, bait shop, fireworks stand and general store with everything from beer to fan belts. A sign on the door noted the prices to be paid for milk, bread and armed robbery. The milk and bread were reasonable. Armed robbery was a minimum of ten years making license plates, ten hours a day, and razor-sharp shivs during spare time.

Crackheads itched and fretted in the bushes while waiting for tourists to stop in so they could rob them. The crackheads rarely got more than a hundred bucks and were sure to get caught eventually. But that didn't stop them. They could always get dope in jail.

It was a great place to make a scene, Mike thought. The driveway was deep sand and the parking lot was paved with used roofing shingles. If Mike could lay off the gas just a little, and if Christy could get just one finger on the door handle… Surely they wouldn't shoot them dead right there in front of God and everybody.

Mike's chest felt like somebody inside was beating his way out with a sledgehammer. Harelip poked him hard with the pistol. "N'urn in," he said.

Mike and Christy soon found themselves in a grubby motel room, handcuffed together, the chain running between the spokes of a twenty-dollar-a-night bedstead.

They never knew for sure what had gone down. More than likely the men were cops who had busted the coke dealer, taken his stash and were reading him his rights when he said, "Hey, wait a minute, officers. A couple of guys with a wad of cash are on their way over ..."

The dealer lost his stash but probably walked.

Mike and Christy sat on the cold concrete floor, their backs to Masonite paneling, and waited. And waited.

After a while, the short man stuck his head in the door with a bit of kindly advice: "Don't you EVER let us catch your crusty asses in Charleston County again."

The harelip let a single twenty flutter to the bed. "Ga'th for your truck. N'you need N'ome."

Mike and Christy waited until they heard two car doors slam and the white Ford with black tires and silver-moon hubcaps peel off onto the highway.

Then they started kicking. They kicked the bed frame, kicked the mattress. They kicked each other. They kicked loose one bed board spoke, then another. They kicked each other some more. They kicked until their wrists and ankles bled.

Finally there was enough room for Mike to squeeze through the bedstead, and soon they stood there side-by-side in the cheap motel room sweating, breathless and free, except from each other.

"Jesus Christ," Mike panted. "I thought we was a goner."

Christy managed a weak grin.

Together, they found the single towel in the bathroom, wrapped it around the chain and walked outside like they were holding hands. The crackheads watched from the bushes as they both got into the truck on the driver's side. Obviously, they weren't right in the head, so the crackheads let them go.

"I got a hacksaw and some cold chisels in my garage," Mike said. "Let's go home."

About forty-five minutes later, as the blackwater Ashepoo gave way to the brackish brown Combahee, Christy asked, "Hey man, ever rolled a joint with cuffs on?"

"Hold the wheel," Mike said.

TWENTY FOUR

Poogey Drake should have known something was up when his wife didn't come home for Thanksgiving. She always came for Thanksgiving. But Poogey's embers of suspicion got lost in the glare of his surroundings. He was getting plenty of sex from three women, sometimes two at a time if he paid extra for it. One way or the other, he always had to pay.

Susan, yes Susan, God bless her. He hoped she was happy. But Charlene and Debbie and what's-her-name with the boa constrictor tattooed up her right shoulder took care of business for him. He was fine with everything so long as nothing reared up and bit him in the ass. Just the thought of being humiliated, especially in public, made him reach for his Pepsid.

Poogey Drake met Sam at the Masters golf tournament the year great mobs of Yankee matrons descended upon Georgia to protest Augusta National's male-only policy. Humorless, bedraggled, shapeless women coveyed up in knots of a dozen or so outside the gates, standing grimly with illegible signs washed out by the deluge that postponed the tourney for half a day. The azalea blooms hung their heads, sheding rainwater like tears.

"What you think, Sam?" Poogey had asked as they squished through the rough toward the fourth tee. Poogey wore two-toned shoes and his socks were wet. "We could make Daufuskie Island an international golf destination. Want a drink, Sam?"

They elbowed their way under the kiosk, where Poogey bought two scotches and a couple of egg-salad sandwiches and they walked clear of the crowd. "And ferry it all over?" Sam asked.

Poogey gulped from his green plastic commemorative cup. He drank a lot for years and he quit for years, and now he was drinking a lot again. He could feel the liquor before it landed in his stomach. "We'll hire horses and carriages, dress the drivers up in swallowtail coats. This could be Williamsburg on the Water."

Sam raised his cup to his lips, then let it down without taking a sip. "They got golf at Williamsburg?"

Poogey took another slug and snapped his fingers. "Exactly."

That's how it all started. Sam said he wanted to see the property. Poogey chartered the plane and a pilot who flew them over the island and changed everything.

That was last summer; it was late fall now. Poogey Drake was in Atlanta and his wife was still on the island and nothing was blooming – nothing except Susan Drake and the potted gardenia in her living room. It was a hybrid, local stock grafted to a South African exotic. She couldn't remember its name. Poogey bought it for her one night just before he came home late and drunk. She brought it to the island in the back seat of her new Mercedes.

She loved that gardenia. It was fertile. She set it in a window facing the sea and talked to it every morning over coffee. It bushed out and bore blossoms May through November.

And now Yancey had picked the last blossom of the season and he was with her in her canopy bed and he painted her with its fragrance. He began below her chin and with broad strokes worked down, nosing along behind, sniffing the scent like a hound. She closed her eyes and smiled.

Yancey and Susan stayed together nearly every night. She gave him a golf cart with a Daufuskie Island Club and Resort sticker on the windshield so he would waste no time at the gate. The guards huffed and paced, but the sticker was as good as gold.

She would take Yancey at the hour of her choosing. Sometimes he took her at his. But however and whenever one would take the other, he'd wait until the last boat left before he dared to fall asleep. And he always got home before the morning boat came in. After a couple of months of this, all her coffee cups were at his house, all his whisky glasses at hers.

So Susan Drake did not go home for Thanksgiving. Yancey figured he had about six months left before they got caught. There was plenty of traceable evidence: Curious guards at the gate with stubby lead pencils; his name when he signed tabs on her club card; boat logs when he went for groceries and liquor; phone logs if anybody took the trouble to get them; Chip, Jimmie, Johnny, Sherida and Cassandra – they all knew.

Susan was ill that morning, rushing often to the toilet and retching. He gave her a moment and brought a cool washrag for her forehead and a glass of water to rinse her mouth. As he resumed tracing her belly with the gardenia and tracking the scent, she said quietly, "I might be pregnant."

Yancey had his first brush with paternity in a singlewide near Hardeeville. He was likkered up real good in the bedroom and a hell of a party was going on just outside the door. The other guests thumped off walls and tripped over the furniture. Jimmy Hendrix blared up a purple haze while Yancey gazed into the girl's bright brown eyes and fondled her tiny breasts. She was better than nothing. Soon after the baby arrived, she had the same bright brown eyes and bigger breasts and the cops hauled in seven men for blood tests. But they never called Yancey.

Years afterward, he occasionally wished they had. It saddened him to think of a baby girl without a daddy to love, to teach her how to cast a net and heave a surf rod, to shoot a deer rifle. He thought maybe someday a pretty fourteen-year-old would show up on his porch and say, "Daddy?"

Yancey read in the Good Book where it said a man who destroys the faith of a child should have a millstone tied around his neck and be thrown into the sea. He'd seen plantation millstones – thick granite disks with grooves for grinding wheat to flour and corn to grits. The Gullahs who did the grinding were gone now and the old stones lay here and there in litters of leaves in the woods. Nobody stole them – too heavy. He'd treat that child like his daughter, even if she were not. That's what he thought.

Now he had traced Susan all the way down to her belly with that gardenia bloom, and he asked, "What you want to call her?"

Susan Drake had been born and raised in Atlanta and had seen *Gone with the Wind* three times when she was little. She didn't swoon when Rhett kissed Scarlet, she didn't weep when he left, she didn't stand up and throw popcorn at the screen when the Yankees came, or shake her fist and cuss them like her momma did. But she did marry a man who built her a big brick house with a broad veranda and tall white columns like hundreds of others that sprang up in Georgia after General Sherman cleared out and Coca-Cola moved in.

"Tara," she said.

Oh Great God, Yancey thought. "Uh-uh," he said.

"What, then?" she asked.

Yancey looked out the window at the surf rolling up on the beach. It was the redfish season – when big-hog spot-tail bass hit cut mullet and fight like hell. They clean easy and eat good. But Yancey could not think about big bass right now. It sounded like maybe Susan knew about Tara Lynn, so he had to think fast: "Talledega," he said. "It's Indian for something."

Talladega was where one of the last battles in the Confederate War was fought in Alabama. Talladega is the name of the town and of the NASCAR racetrack, too. Though he'd never been there, he liked the way it rolled off his tongue.

She smiled. "Talladega? Little Talley Yarboro? I like that."

Yancey dropped the flower and stretched out beside her. She propped up on one elbow. The windows were open and she pulled up the covers against the November breeze.

"She'll be tall like me and blonde like you," he said. "She'll be a smart little skutter, with neon-blue eyes and a face full of freckles."

"We'll buy a cradle," Susan said.

"A tomato crate will do," Yancey said. "One with Yarboro Farms printed on each end. I'll varnish it and make a foam mattress to fit."

"Where will she go to school?"

"In Bluffton. I'll run her over in the skiff."

"Every day?"

"Good weather and bad," he said.

"First we'll home-school her for a few years."

"Yeah," Yancey said. "Basic and Advanced Deer Skinning. Oyster Picking. Surf Casting. Coon Hunting."

"We'll get her some white rubber shrimper boots and a teeny-weeny lifejacket."

"When she's thirteen, she can drive the boat herself."

"Can she do that?"

"Yes ma'am," he said. "Even better than me."

Yancey closed his eyes and he could see the girl sitting amidships, little boots on her feet, legs dangling but not long enough to reach the bottom boards, river wind blowing wisps of her hair around the edges of her yellow slicker hood, eyes bright and wide with wonder as they buzzed around switchback bends in Bull River. *God, what a beautiful child!*

"You'll be a good momma," he said.

"And you'll be a great father."

"I'll be so proud of both of you."

Susan Drake laughed, but felt like crying. "Come here to me, Mister."

Yancey seldom cried, but he came close just then as he slid beneath the covers and buried his bumpy nose between her breasts. She smelled like jasmine perfume with a trace of gardenia. And cigarettes, whisky and tuna, too – all of which whooshed up his nostrils and exploded across his brain like a twenty-dollar skyrocket.

Later when they were breathless and spent, she slipped out of bed and into a long slinky thing. Yancey did not know what to call it. Looked like silk, maybe nylon, and it reached her knees and clung to her curves and showed everything better than if she'd been stark naked. She headed for the bathroom again, saying over her shoulder, "You know, I can never have children."

# TWENTY FIVE

"We ought to give some money to the Democrats," Christy said.

"You been smoking too much dope." Mike shook his head. "Why not the Republicans?"

"You a damn Republican?"

"No," Mike replied. "Republicans are a virus."

"You got that right, man."

"And Democrats are a bacteria," Mike added.

Christy and Mike were almost full partners but Christy was still boss because he had more money and he was smarter. They were at Christy's condo, smoking reefer, sucking down beers and strategizing. It was ten in the morning.

The cell phone was working again and Christy had been up most of the night, talking back and forth with a trawler captain coming up from Panama. Cap'um Jack was out of the picture now, paid off and gone looking for Sondra, who had run off somewhere with some cokehead.

"Clinton smoked dope," Christy observed.

"But he lied about it."

"Of course he lied. The whole damn government is a lie and he was the President," Christy said, blowing a smoke ring at Mike. "They say smoking reefer will make you run out and rob a filling station, throw your payment book in the river and screw your neighbor's wife."

"Two out of three ain't bad," Mike said.

Christy grinned. "Yeah, but that ain't the point."

"What is?"

"Making money. Bottom line is we ain't no worse than them."

Mike pondered that for a couple of seconds, then said, "So long as we keep our asses out of Charleston County."

"They weren't gonna kill nobody for no two thousand bucks," Christy said.

"Could have fooled me."

Christy grinned, shook his head, rolled up another joint. They had so much dope now that they didn't bother to pass them back and forth. They rolled them thick and held them in their teeth and smoked them with no hands and left fat roaches smoldering in ashtrays like they were Bull Durhams. "But we got loose, didn't we?"

"Damn near didn't."

"Hey man, that's just the way this business is," Christy said. "A miss is as good as a mile. I ever tell you about the cocaine plane?"

"Which one?"

"Over on Daufuskie twelve years ago. They found a plane. They found what was left of the pilot. They found his personal stash and a thousand bucks. But they never found the load."

Mike whistled. "Gone?"

"Yeah, man, gone. They found footprints and motorcycle tracks all around the crash site."

"Somebody come up on a dirt bike and stole the load?"

"Yep, and there was only one motorcycle on the island back then."

"Shouldn't a been hard to figure out."

"But they never did."

"Yarboro," Mike said.

"Nope."

"Who, then?"

"Damned if I know. They said it was some real estate man. He built himself a damn fine house over there about six months later."

"I'd put my money on Yarboro. That's probably what those burglars were after when his daddy killed them."

"Well, maybe, but you think he'd still be farming tomatoes if it was him?"

"Reckon not," Mike said. He paused. "Look here, how long you think we can get away with this smuggling shit?"

Christy made an X with his two index fingers and held them up in front his face like he was fending off a vampire. "Quit talking like that, man."

"I'm dead-ass serious," Mike said. "We gonna get caught any time soon?"

"You want to go back to pulling crab pots?"

"Hell, no!"

"Maybe Yarboro will give you a job picking tomatoes," Christy said as he opened a kitchen drawer and pulled out a pair of binoculars. They were big expensive European glasses, the kind you see U-boat captains wearing around their necks in old war movies. Christy walked to the patio and eyed the river, all crinkly and blue on a late-November morning. "I can tell you a couple of things," he said over his shoulder. "If we get nailed, we won't know where it came from, and it'll be for what we do, not for what we did."

"How's that?"

"There's just no connection, man. We got clean away with the first load and we're about to get clean away with another. Just like whoever it was that got away with the cocaine after the plane when down."

"When's the boat due?" Mike asked.

"He's ten miles off Ossabaw, he'll clear the bar at sundown," Christy said as he returned to the living room and plopped in his chair. "You worried?"

"Been scared shitless since we hooked up at the fish house."

Christy laughed. "I mean, what have we really done? Talk on the phone? Walk around with a suitcase full of money?"

"Conspiracy," Mike said. "Tax evasion. Don't forget us toting that shit over to Daufuskie and back."

"Yeah," Christy said, taking another hit and grinning. "But nobody knows but us."

"Yarboro knows," Mike said.

Christy rolled his eyes. "Him again? What's eating you?"

"He's a bad-ass."

"Maybe he is, but we didn't have any trouble with him, now did we? Listen, I'll make you a promise. Ain't no dope worth doing time. Even if we beat the rap, lawyers will eat up the profit and the IRS will dog us forever. So, any heat, and we'll scoot – right off the radar screen." Christy swept his arm out. "Right off the pages of history."

"Right off the pages?"

"Yeah, man."

"Then what?"

"You can quit if you want," Christy said. "I'll slide up the coast a ways." He paused, then added, "And start all over again, just like last time. But first, I'll commission us a statue."

"A statue? To who?"

"To us."

"And you talking about dropping off the page."

Christy's eyes lit up and he wagged a finger at Mike. "Yeah, we'll call it the Unknown Smuggler."

"Like it," Mike said.

"Think about everybody who smokes our dope, all them people we make happy. We're heroes, man. We'll set that smuggling sonofabitch up downtown at Waterfront Park!"

"Will they let us do that?"

"You ever seen Beaufort turn down free art? They put up a bunch of plastic cows on the street corners, you know," Christy said.

"Plastic cows? Why?"

"Because they were free! The Unknown Smuggler will be younger than us," Christy elaborated, "and he'll be all worried-looking, staring out to sea."

"In bronze forever," Mike said.

"No man, stone. Stoned in stone," Christy snickered and took another toke.

"I like it, I like it," Mike said. "Pupils like B-B's, the wind in his hair and a walkie-talkie in his hand. Shotgun at his feet."

"Yeah, man, an *unloaded* shotgun," Christy chortled. "We'll get us a plaque that says: *To the Unknown Smuggler.*

"Yeah, *Neither threat of incarceration ...*" Mike started.

"*... or assassination ...*" Christy continued.

"*... or honest police,*" Mike said. "Is it *nor?*"

"Damned if I know, but we ought to get it right. *Or crooked police ... Nor tropical storms ...*"

"*Can keep these couriers from their appointed rounds,*" finished Mike.

Christy slapped his thigh. "Hot damn, man, you got it!"

Christy's cell phone began playing the first bars of the Star Spangled Banner, *Oh say, can you see*, over and over. It took him a while to find it.

"Uh-huh," Christy said into the phone, followed by a pause. "No problem, I'll have somebody meet you. Hang off the sea buoy till sundown." He snapped the cover shut.

"What?" Mike asked.

"Idiot came all the way from Panama and now he wants a freaking pilot to bring him in. You run offshore and meet him, idle him across the bar, get him to the island."

"Me?" Mike said.

"Why not?"

"But you said if there's any heat, we'll haul ass."

"We can," Christy said. "And we will."

"How in hell am I gonna haul ass way out there by the buoy? Jump overboard?"

"Somebody's got to do it. Remember what that bastard Jack did?"

Mike sat silent for a moment. "Yarboro," he said.

"Yarboro?"

"Hell yes, Yarboro! He don't live five miles away."

Christy snapped his fingers. "I'll give our boy a call. Grab me another brew."

TWENTY SIX

Yancey sat in a law office in a strip-mall alongside U.S. 278. Years ago, the highway was just Buckingham Road, a two-lane mainland blacktop down to Buckingham Ferry Landing through a tunnel of live oaks. But the oaks are gone and there's a huge concrete bridge where there used to be a six-car ferry. The road is four lanes in some places, six in others, and the traffic crawls along, bumper to bumper most days.

He waited forty-five minutes while the girl behind the desk took call after call and noted them in a register she kept by the phone. There was a print of the red-and-white striped Morris Island Lighthouse on the wall. Morris Island had all but washed away and the lighthouse – surrounded by surf now – was dark, windblown and leaning. The print was one of a limited edition offered by the Friends of the Morris Island Light, a non-profit raising money to study ways to save it. The prints sold for a thousand bucks each and rich people bought them to prove how much they really cared.

The girl was pretty enough, but she had big feet and walked around the office like a slew. "You got it wrong, Miss," Yancey finally said. "A lawyer ain't likely to talk to you when you don't give him money, but I gave him money damn near an hour ago."

"I'm sorry, Mr. Yarboro," she said, her mouth looking like an old-time pop-open coin purse. "He's still in conference with a client."

There were copies of *Ducks Unlimited* on the end tables and the couch cushions were deep and comfortable. The surf engulfed the base of the Morris Island light, ranks of waves like grieving sea angels tearing out their hair and flinging it to the wind. Traffic rumbled constantly down the highway outside.

This was the day after Yancey got the call from Christy and took the skiff around the north end of Daufuskie an hour before sundown. It was fine and wonderful after he got through the surf and into the heaving sea. The islands soon were off in the distance – long green smudges stretching south all the way to the Florida Keys. Great schools of baitfish surfaced here and there, looking like dark clouds, flashing sliver around the edges where bigger fish shredded them like meat grinders. Birds wheeled and screamed, dipping into the chop, picking up scraps.

The trawler was a hundred-and-fifty-foot steel deep-water job, angular and rusty, and was waiting right where she was supposed to be, just off the red buoy outside the bar. The nets were trailing over the sides like she had just come in from a long haul. Yancey circled once and read the name on her stern, *Angelique,* Port Everglades, Florida. He waved at the skipper, and when the skipper waved back, he headed up the channel at quarter throttle – just a fisherman coming home, just a shrimper following him.

Around Daufuskie, across Calibogue, up May River they went and about nightfall, Yancey idled them by the Pine Island dock. The skipper came out of the wheelhouse and tossed a plastic sandwich bag. *Fwop.* It landed in the bilge at Yancey's feet. He wound up the throttle, and a half-mile later, idled down and opened the bag. Inside were a couple of buds the size of his thumb and ten tattered hundred-dollar bills with Ben Franklin smirking like it was all a big joke.

Damn, that was easy money, Yancey thought while sitting in the law office after giving it all to the lawyer.

Law offices are like whore houses. They have more back doors than front ones. Mr. Wilton K. Ramsey, Esquire, must have forgotten about Yancey Yarboro, or maybe he figured Yancey had given up. The lawyer stepped into the hall and was heading for the front door when Yancey hailed him. Ramsey gurgled, grumbled and snorted like a wild boar when it winds you in a thicket. He was a bilious old barrister who talked like he gargled with castor oil.

Yancey brushed past the secretary. "You've got a thousand dollars of my money," he said to Ramsey.

"This ain't a drive-in restaurant, son." Ramsey's tie was loose and his sleeves rolled up and he had a stack of papers under one arm. "You already got three hours of my time. My convenience, not yours."

"I'm a little short on convenience these days," Yancey said.

Ramsey cocked one eye in his direction. It was bloodshot and as big as a bull's. "On patience, too, I suspect."

"Lost it in a war," Yancey said. "You said you might help me."

"You said you might give me five thousand dollars."

"I just gave you a grand."

Ramsey, feigning great weariness, pulled out a handkerchief and mopped his brow even though he wasn't sweating. "I told you your options were few. I can't pull any crap on the court. Hell, I am an officer of the court."

"The court's got enough officers already," Yancey said. "I need you to work for me."

Wilton K. Ramsey, Esquire, grinned. It was an honest one. "You don't understand, boy. You want me to rage right in there like the wrath of God? I was like you once."

"What happened?"

"They call it wisdom, son. Comes with dental work and full-cut britches."

"Comes from eating too good and sitting on your ass," Yancey said.

"Mr. Yarboro, exactly what is it you hope to accomplish? You bust in here with not enough money and no plan at all and you want me to stop a sale of land over there on that island. The court will see it for exactly what it is."

"And what's that?"

"You attempting to enrich yourself at your father's expense. The court will ask the same question I do: If you are concerned about your father's welfare, why aren't you taking care of him in his infirmity? Why are you hiding over there on that God-forsaken place?"

"My island ain't God-forsaken," Yancey said. "Besides, they told me you could bullshit water uphill."

"They did, did they?" Ramsey laughed and the veins on his nose flashed red and blue. "That's good. I might put it on my business card." He checked his watch. "Look, I've got a two o'clock tee time and I'm not going to make it. So long as you are going to make me late, we might as well have a drink."

Ramsey opened the door to his left and they walked into a dimly lit conference room with more prints of local seascapes and a picture of a birddog getting onto a covey of quail with a plaque thanking Mr. Wilton K. Ramsey, Esquire, for his generous support of Quail Unlimited. There was a long table with chairs all around, and a decanter with two glasses and two cloth napkins on a tray.

Yancey sat down first.

Ramsey poured two healthy shots, slid one Yancey's way. No water, no ice. He squeezed himself into a chair across the table. "Your daddy still has a lot of friends. Ain't likely we'll get an incompetency ruling, you know."

Yancey took a sip. It wasn't as good as Young Heaven Hill. "I figured as much," he said.

"And even if we did, there's still your momma. She'd throw you off the place."

"I figured that, too," Yancey said. "She'd do it in a heartbeat."

"Well, a little longer than that. The sheriff will serve you papers and you'll have sixty days to clear out." Ramsey paused. "But I just thought of something," he said. "Can you get me a nigger graveyard?"

Yancey had never liked that word, and he'd been hearing it since Day One. The Gullahs *niggered* each other all the time, but Yancey used it only when no other word fit. Yet it sat nasty on his tongue just the same. The Judge pegged it perfectly. "They worked for us when they had to," he said, "and then they took care of us when they didn't have too. Always treat a colored man better than a white one, son."

Yancey did just that, saying yes sir and yes ma'am to them, loaning them what little money he had, opening doors for them and letting them through in traffic, whenever he was in traffic, which wasn't often.

"Sure," he said to Ramsey. "I got a nigger graveyard."

Ramsey smiled. "What's it like?"

Yancey figured Ramsey had that angle cornered from the get-go, but would not speak of it until the money shook it loose. But that was what lawyering was all about. So he shrugged and said, "Like most of them, I reckon. All grown up in bushes."

"Old?"

"Clear back to slave times."

"Good. Any stones?"

"A few."

Ramsey thought a minute. "I may not be able to stop 'em, but I can sure as hell shake some wind from their sails. I got a niece in the Department of Archives and History up in Columbia. We'll get the state to order up a survey."

"Already got more surveying than I can stand," Yancey said.

"Let me tell you, son, you ain't seen surveying yet!" Ramsey rubbed his fat palms together and grinned. "They'll mark off ten acres in three-foot squares and dig a post hole in every one. They'll sift through the dirt real careful. If they find anything, which they will, they'll dig some more. There's a formula. If they find more, they'll dig and sift, dig and sift, dig and find, dig up the whole south end of the island, eventually. Meanwhile, borrowed money is drawing interest and the contractors are standing around blowing hot air out their asses. Archaeology! It's a dirty word to developers, son. They hate it more than anything."

Gator Brown, Gator Brown, Yancey thought. *You sly bastard.*

Ramsey nodded toward the bottle and Yancey livened up their glasses again, even though he had a tide to catch. This was too damned good. But he should have remembered what the Good Book says: "Pride cometh before a fall."

"It'll take six months and cost 'em a hundred grand, and of course they won't find much of anything real important, a few bones and some buttons maybe. I'll need more money," Ramsey said, "and I'll need the name and address of the chief executive officer of the corporation."

"What corporation?"

Ramsey harrumphed and gurgled some more. "Why Daufuskie Island Investments, the one holding the option on your daddy's land."

Yancey about choked. The top of his skull bulged and his brain felt like a water balloon somebody had squeezed from the bottom. "Option! What option?"

"Mr. Yarboro, Daufuskie Island Investments has a ninety-day option on that land." He glanced up at a calendar. "Make that sixty-two."

"Why didn't you tell me?"

"You just paid me and I just did," Ramsey said. "They have another two months for 'due diligence'. If the title ain't clear by then, if something is fixing to jump up and bite 'em in the butt, they can back out with no penalty."

"More money!" Yancey sprang to his feet as his chair tipped back on two legs and clattered down again.

"Thanks for the drink!" Yancey said, and he was about to quote the Good Book, all on his own this time, *"Woe unto ye, ye lawyers, ye vipers, ye hypocrites."* But since Wilton K. Ramsey, Esquire, was his viper now, Yancey figured he'd best leave scripture out of it.

"I reckon you bought that drink, son. Now get me that name."

"Can't your girl get it?"

Ramsey finished his drink, smacked his lips. "Sure she can, but it will cost you a hundred bucks. Just go to the state website."

"Website?" Yancey asked.

"Don't you have a computer, son?"

"I'm lucky I got a phone," Yancey said.

"You *do* have a phone book?"

"I got one."

"Call up the Secretary of State's office. It's in the blue pages."

"And you'll bullshit water uphill?"

"You need more than that, son. You need Moses to part the sea."

"If I had Moses, I wouldn't need no lawyer," Yancey said.

 # TWENTY SEVEN

Yancey wanted to be in love, more than he had thought he was when he'd fought over Tara Lynn. But with Susan Drake it was not as easy as busting some greaser in the head with a beer bottle and getting his ass kicked by the redneck's buddies. Yancey found he was fighting *with* Susan as well as *for* her.

"You lied to me," he said.

She stood in the doorway, eager for him until she saw the look on his face – a *'struction* look, as the Gullah say, as in "de-struction."

"You lied, dammit, you lied," he repeated.

Susan had dreaded this. She had looked for the right moment to tell him, perhaps on a glorious morning when they were watching the sun come up over the sea, or on some moonlit night when the sea turtles were crawling up to lay eggs in the dunes, or a lazy afternoon when he was drifting off to sleep in her arms. She had wanted to tell him but she could not find the words, and now she saw his wildness, which she loved so much, turn to fury.

Behind her were ranks of her black-and-white prints on hardwood easels – seascapes, sea oats and shells. They were good enough to sell, but now they seemed to Yancey as lifeless as the tombstones in the old Gullah burying ground. There was even a picture of him, looking out to sea with a wry smile.

"Did you ever think that I might be in a position to help?" she began. Her heart was breaking, too.

"Would that be the missionary position?" Yancey snarled, his pulse roaring like surf in his ears.

"And just what do you mean by that?"

She and Yancey had used up every point of the compass – in the bed, on the beach, in the woods, in the golf cart, in the pool, in the clubhouse bathroom over the sink, in the boat, on the bow of the ferry, at the stern of the ferry, in the head of the ferry, in the truck, even once under the truck. She had been like that with Poogey in the beginning, but bedded him now only on rare occasions, and always in the missionary position, just like Yancey said. She knew that Yancey could not know the details of her private life with Poogey. He had just guessed, but still it cut her to the bone.

"You lied to me," he said once more. "I been sleeping with the enemy and didn't know it."

"I have never lied to you," she hissed, "and I am not your enemy."

"Bullshit. You never told me the truth! You lied with your lips and your hands and your ..." He stopped himself short.

"I'm going home," she said.

"You said this was home. You said this was my house just like it was yours."

"Maybe I thought it was. Maybe I was wrong. I'm going home to Atlanta."

"Well go on, then. Go on home and blow your old man!" Yancey was shouting now. "And tell him to turn my land a-loose! Excuse me, I forgot, you can't talk with your mouth full."

He regretted saying that as she recoiled as if he had slapped her.

"I'm sorry, honey." He moved toward her.

Her fist came out of nowhere and landed solidly on his upper jaw and ear. Her arm was long and her knuckles hard and Yancey rocked back on his heels and nearly went down. His left ear rang like a church bell and spangles of red and green exploded across his eyes.

"Why don't you call me something you've never called another woman!" she screamed.

He remembered the time he was standing naked at the sink, his chest and arms slick with soapy dishwater, and she had slipped up behind him with a butcher knife and feigned to cut his throat. He had smiled and tilted back his head to make it easier for her. That's how much he had trusted her then.

"How about *Puta?*" he said, spitting out the *P.*

Susan Drake knew some Spanish too, and she hit him again, with the back of her hand this time. Yancey slid to his knees and rocked back and forth, holding his head in his hands. His left ear felt like somebody had run an ice pick down it.

"Dammit!" he said. "At least you could've hit me on the other side."

She just stood there, and from his other ear Yancey heard her sobbing.

"I fixed the son of a bitch good," he said without looking up. "I got a lawyer and he sicced the state archaeologist on him. They'll be digging up bones for a long time."

She was silent for a minute. "What do you need me for?" she asked through her tears.

"Nothing," he said. "Not a damn thing."

"I'm going home," she said.

Yancey left her golf cart in her driveway and walked to the back of the island, his part of the island. The woods were lovely this time of year, the oak leaves thinned out and the underbrush bare and the water trees aflame in red and gold. But he had no eye for them, and though the woods had dried up and the walking was easy, he trudged along as if each shoe were caked with ten pounds of swamp mud.

Later he stood on his dock and watched her walk down to the ferry and step aboard. He saw her greet the captain and the mate and she waved her hands around the way she always did when she talked to men. He saw her throw back her head and laugh. Yancey was too far away to hear what she was saying to them. The captain fired the engines and the deckhands dropped the lines. The stack belched a puff of black smoke and the Daufuskie Island Ferry pulled out into the booming ebb tide.

The captain swung the boat down-tide and idled past him about two hundred yards out. She stood on the fantail and he stood on his dock and they looked at each other across the widening water. She lit a cigarette and blew smoke in his direction and the sea wind blew it back in her face.

He stood there with his hands in his pockets and a pain in his heart, his ear still ringing like a brass bell. She raised one long, tanned and lovely leg and dangled it over the railing and gazed at him like she was ready to jump overboard if he would do the same. But he did not and she did not and the water between them got wider and wider and then she was gone.

The phone was ringing when Yancey got back inside. It wasn't quite the same sound as the noise in his ear. He didn't hear it all at first. He let it ring a while, hoping whoever was on the other end would go away.

The phone line stretched over six miles of marsh and under four creeks and three rivers. They had strung it back during the war so the Coast Guard could call in if they spotted any Germans slipping ashore. Somebody snagged the line with an anchor about the time Yancey was born and nobody bothered to replace it until the resort came along forty years later. But still, it wasn't much of a line. The phones popped and crackled like a Sears and Roebuck door buzzer.

"Heartbreak Hotel," Yancey said when he finally picked up the phone.

There was a long pause.

"Yarboro?" It was Mike but Yancey could barely make him out, his ear ringing like it was and the connection crackling too.

He switched ears. "Yeah, this is Yarboro. What?"

"Our skipper take good care of you?"

"Yeah," Yancey said, "pretty good."

"Want some more?"

"Same-same?"

"No man, we got trouble with the off-load. Need to hump bales."

Yancey didn't mind piloting the trawler across the bar and up the sound. Nothing to it. But this was different. "How much?"

"Ten thousand," Mike said. "Dusk to dawn."

And so Yancey Yarboro, who had nothing more to lose, did not say yes. He said hell yes.

TWENTY EIGHT

"I done been tole you, don' come round yeah if you ain' wan' her no mo'," Gator Brown said.

It was a mouthful. An earful, too. *Done been tole* was Gullah past perfect tense, and there is nothing quite like it in Standard English. It's African, past and entirely perfect: *I have emphatically spoken with you repeatedly about it a very long time ago.*

They were sitting on Gator Brown's front porch. Popeye, the one-eyed wonder dog, lay on the floor between them, eyeballing a dark gathering beneath the trees at the edge of the yard and gnawing at an occasional flea like somebody eating corn on the cob.

The pecan tree had shed its nuts, and then its leaves, but great tattered ghosts of moss hung on. The tree stood stalwart in the yard, its limbs like arms raised up in resignation as if to say: *Boy, I done been seen it all, earthquake and storm and slave and war and pirate; shootin' an cuttin' and bad likka dat drive men crazy blind. I done been seen generations sprung up an' cut down like grass and shrowed in de fire. But, boy, I ain' seen nothin' like you. What you done now?*

Gator Brown had battled with nature and come out with a couple of pounds of shelled nuts and two dozen squirrels for the pot. Yancey had not been so fortunate.

"I do want her," he said.

Gator snorted. "Lucky she ain' cut you up, callin' her how you did."

"Reckon so," Yancey said. "Don't know what got into me."

"How you know dat Portygee?"

"Spanish, not Portuguese." Yancey said. "It's Spanish from my Mexicans. They talk *puta* all the time."

"I tole you dat gal worse den dope and likka togedda."

Yancey shook his head. "You just said gal, not that gal."

"Don't dispute wid ol' Gator." He fixed on Yancey with a long and crooked finger. "Dat gal be gal."

"Sho' nuff is," Yancey said, his accent changing.

Talking with Gator Brown was almost like having a conversation with yourself. He looked at you like he couldn't quite figure how to ask a question but like he already knew what the answer was. Yancey did not have any answers.

He had jumped into his skiff about sundown and headed for Pine Island. He brought along his Coleman lamp, his gig and his foot tub, just like he was going to ride the ebb tide home and stick flounder after dark. It was a good way to get fish in a hurry, especially way down in the fall when you can thump on the bottom of the boat with a paddle and call up a porpoise.

Thump, thump, thump. Then way out in the creek – *kawoosh* – you could hear that porpoise snort, then it would ride the tide beside you and run the fish from deep water up onto the mud bank where you could stab at them with a gig. If you missed and the fish headed back to deep water, the porpoise would get a crack at them, too. Yancey had also brought his work gloves. He had some lifting to do.

Angelique lay alongside the dock dark and deserted like a lonely woman in the half-light. Way overhead the evening Delta flight from D.C. rumbled and whined into Savannah. Yancey idled along with the tide and turned things over in his mind as he neared the port side of the trawler. He also wondered where the crew was. Just as the skiff bumped up against the trawler, somebody stuck an M-16 in Yancey's face. Yancey knew it was an M-16. He had learned all about them at Fort Jackson. He saw movement, a head and part of a shoulder, just a blur actually, but he knew the gun: stiletto barrel, slotted flash-hider held up against the light of the leaden sky. Most other men would have raised their hands and hollered, "Hey! I'm just out here gigging fish!"

Yancey had been shot at and missed and he had been shot at and hit. He'd had knives to his neck, and a shotgun at his nose. There was no time to think at that particular moment, so he reached up, grabbed the muzzle and snatched down hard.

The man on the other end of the gun did not let go at first, and Yancey jerked him off the side of the trawler, catapulting him over the skiff and into the water.

The gun cut loose in full auto: *Bop-a-bop-a-bop-a.*

The muzzle flash lit up the air like it was the Fourth of July and the shell casings flew by Yancey's head and rattled around in the bottom of the boat. It sounded like he had run up on an oyster bank. He hit the throttle and cut for deep water.

There was a lot of hollering above from the deck. Whatever was left of Yancey's hearing was gone now, and between the ringing in his ears and the whine of the boat motor, he could not make out the words.

Sounded sort of like, "Stop! Stop, or we'll shoot!"

But they were busy fishing their man out of the river and they had already started shooting, so Yancey kept on going.

Bop-a-bop-a-bop-a. Another burst and the bullets whizzed by his head. And then there were a few scattered shots, closer now, and then a whang and a whine as a slug ricocheted off the motor case.

Yancey slid off the seat and hunched down low in the bilge. Water blubbered up through the bottom and it was damn cold on his nubbins. He kept his head down and wrung the throttle until his fingers hurt.

Pop, pop, pop – more shots as he rounded the first bend in Bull River, out of range.

The skiff was taking water – little geysers spraying up through the bottom. Bullet holes – one, two, three, four. He throttled back and the bow rose and the first two holes came clear of the wake. The others were far astern so he pulled the drain plug in the transom and let the water run out as fast as it came in. If I can keep her off a sandbar, he thought, she'll keep on going.

Yancey knew the river, in daylight and dark, and he was not likely to hit a shoal. But about the time he dared show his head above the gunnels, he saw it. Damn, he said to himself, here comes the blue-light special.

He could see the strobe flashing above the spartina grass. The sea mist caught the light and made a blue cloud each time it came around – *flash, flash* – getting closer. And then he saw the M-16, which landed with a clatter Yancey did not hear near the bow of his boat. The flash-hider peeked from under the forward seat.

On the south bank of Bull River just before it dumped into Calibogue Sound was a side creek that was deep water, even at low tide. It wound around behind a line of shell rakes. Gullah oyster pickers threw shells there years ago, before the sewer and the slop from Savannah poisoned all the oyster beds. The wind and tide piled the shells high along the bank and it was a damn fine spot to lie up and shoot canvass-backs.

Yancey ran up the creek and cut the throttle, jumped overboard into the shallows and pulled the skiff onto the shells. He grabbed the rifle from beneath the seat, dumped the water from the action and checked the chamber. It had been a long time since he had handled an M-16 but he remembered what to do. One round in the chamber, a dozen or so in the magazine. He flipped the fire selector from full auto to burst, which would give him three quick shots each time he pulled the trigger. If they found him, one burst would turn them.

They would return, he knew, with more boats and a helicopter. But when they did they would not find him. He'd quit the boat and slog through the marsh toward the scrubby cedar hummocks between the island and the mainland – the "flying away" places where runaway slaves prayed to be transformed into crows so they could fly home to Africa.

Yancey asked to be an otter instead, sliding on the mud, swimming to freedom.

He knew they would find his boat and the registration numbers would identify him as the owner. He would call as soon as he got to a phone and report it stolen, just like his cousin Eustis did when they found his mosquito-spray plane loaded with dope in the marsh off Brunswick. Smugglers stole planes and boats all the time.

He checked the rifle again, looked down the sights. There was just enough light to see the glint of water where the creek cut back to the west. It would likely be big – eighteen, twenty feet with a center console and twin engines, probably Mercs, which were not even worth government work. She'd throw a bow wave and that would light her up good – a big target, even in the dark. He slipped back into the water and crouched behind the boat and checked the rifle for a third time. And he shivered because it was cold.

But the blue light flashed on down the river and was soon lost in the clutter of lights from Hilton Head – the marinas where he could not afford the gas, the riverside mansions and fancy condos where he could not afford to live, the four-star restaurants where he could not afford to eat.

Damn, that would have been a fine thing, he thought, *to have got some dope on board first. If it weren't for the holes in the boat and me about to piss my pants and freeze to death, I'd be laid up here behind this shell rake in about as good a shape as when this whole thing started.*

So he thought and he wished and he shivered and he waited in case the blue-light special returned. When it did not, he worked his skiff off the shells and crawled aboard. The motor cranked right up, and in about five or six minutes he was in big water again. The mist gathered now to fog, as gray and snuffling as the muzzle of an old deerhound. It was the kind of mist that hovers here and there in steel-wool patches, drifting along in the breeze, tangling in treetops and twisting in the moonlight. Yancey's ears still rang and the copper shard in his brain buzzed. The local shrimpers were anchored out around him, ready to get a jump on the morning trawl. The brown shrimp were running and a dozen boats swung with the tide in halos and rainbows, holy and transcendent like Jesus was walking out there upon the water and saying to them: "Shipworms and bankers gone get you boys by and by, but tonight I'll shine my light on you one last time."

Soon Yancey idled to some live oaks on the east side of the river. The moon was up now and the great limbs threw shadows out over the marsh, and he hid beneath them. The skiff was still taking water. In the dappled moon-shade he could see the holes and he knew he would have to scuttle her. There was a broad scar atop the motor case too, a glancing crease, peeled paint and unraveling fiberglass. *I almost caught that one*, he thought.

Boats were plentiful, but good motors were hard to find – a hundred bucks a horse and he needed at least a hundred horses' worth. *I'll be damned if I'm gonna throw this motor overboard.* So he unhooked the engine, wrestled it ashore and up the bank and into the shed. He returned with an old cultivator, a hunk of rusted steel that used to fit the Ford tractor before he sprung it on a hickory stump.

It was heavy as hell. He dragged it into the boat, untied the line, cast his skiff adrift and watched the tide take it downstream. It would not float for long.

The M-16 was slung over his right shoulder now. It was a military model, select fire, just like the one he had lugged up Drag Ass Hill at the end of each day at Fort Jackson. You might could buy one from the backseat of a Savannah dope dealer's car, but you'd never find one in a pawn shop. Possessing a full auto would get you ten years in the federal slammer. Yancey cursed as he slipped it from his shoulder and flung it as far as he could into the water.

Now he had no woman, no money, no boat, no gun and nobody to turn to but Gator Brown. So that's what Yancey did.

"What you gone do now?" Gator asked as he sat next to Yancey and stared out at the pecan tree.

"Don't know," Yancey said. "I feel like I'm goin' back'ards."

Gator Brown never took his eyes off the tree. "You know what de Good Book say? All *ting* work for good. You oughta get yo' ass to chu'ch."

"I been once or twice. Never seen you."

Gator Brown stroked his dog with one hand, tapped his own forehead with the other. "Me an' Popeye got all de churchin' we need right chere."

The dog worked the porch decking with his tail – *thump, thump* – and way out in the woods, a barred owl was asking a lot of questions in the gathering dark.

TWENTY NINE

Yancey figured he was in trouble. How could he figure otherwise?

Maybe he didn't really steal that gun. Maybe the cop just dropped it. No, they would not see it that way. He could damn near hear it on the evening news: "A suspected drug trafficker assaulted an officer of the law, took his weapon and fled arrest. He is armed and dangerous and still at large here in the Coastal Empire."

They might shoot me down like a dog and I'll gurgle and bleed and die. The Judge and my momma will grieve, but nobody else will, Yancey thought. *Susan Drake – damn her – might take to her bed for a day or two. Might not.*

The newspapers would puzzle over it for a few days, just like when the Judge shot the burglars. But the story would get old and something else would take its place – a murder-suicide or a dreadlocked illegal immigrant sticking up a filling station then fleeing into the street and getting run over by a Mack truck. A child might be found locked in a metal storage shed by his parents, members of some religious cult arrested eating dinner at the Golden Corral Steakhouse.

And after a while two sumbitches would be hooked over their beers down at Sully's and one of them would say, "Hey you remember that crazy Yarboro? Whatever happened to him?"

And after that, nobody would give a shit.

This is what Yancey fretted over. But he knew he had also led what some might call a charmed life, and this gave him hope. He was no prophet, though he longed to be. He damn sure was no prophet's son. He was not even a Seventh Son, enshrined in hoodoo lore. But he still had a way with girls, although now it seemed more of a curse than a blessing. He had a way of ducking bullets, of talking himself out of harm's way, of getting away with stuff that would have put ten other men in the ground.

The cops were over at Hilton Head and surely looking for him now and they didn't even know his name. The rifle was gone, the shot-up boat was sunk and there was hardly anything to connect him with that goat-rope in Bull River. He'd claim the boat was stolen and he would stash the motor in the woods until he found another case. Or he would say he was just another patriotic American veteran with a Chinese bullet lodged in his brain, that he suffered from post-traumatic stress disorder and was trying to gig himself a mess of flounder when somebody stuck a gun in his face and suddenly he was back in a fox hole and didn't know what happened after that.

True, Mike had called him once or twice – probably on a cell phone. But Mike and Christy were running for sure by now. For his own sake, he hoped they got away. Maybe they called when he was out in the river. He did not have an answering machine, so he could not know. Or maybe they figured the cops would run off chasing him, so they'd let him take the heat while they got a head start.

Yancey remembered Hugh Glass, the old mountain man his friends had left to die after he got mauled by a grizzly. Hugh Glass crawled, then hobbled and finally walked until he caught up with his pals in a St. Louis whorehouse. When he had the chance to kill them, he did not, since hating them was the only thing that gave him the strength to survive his trip down the mountain and across the plains. Yancey did not want to spend the rest of his days like that.

He was fixing to hitch up the disc harrow now. In two months, he'd be putting down fertilizer. He had to worry the winter weeds first – the castor bean, nutgrass and cockle, the wild blue indigo, still coming since slave times. But he wasn't in the field yet. It was daybreak on Sunday and Yancey was about halfway through his second cup of coffee and thinking hard about everything he had to do.

Then he noticed a new boat tied to the inside float down at the ferry dock, the kind of boat he did not want to see – a twenty-foot Pro-line skiff, center console, with twin Mercs. There was a big whip aerial on the steering station and a pincushion full of smaller ones on the roof. There was an official-looking insignia on the side but a docking fender hid most of the lettering and the binoculars didn't help.

Game wardens!

Yancey skipped breakfast, a meal he seldom missed. The wardens came over from time to time whenever shrimping got really good. They rented a golf cart from the resort and hid behind the dunes with a video camera and a radio, spotting shrimp-boat captains working too close to shore. If the wardens could snag an island Gullah man right after shooting a deer, picking a bushel of oysters off a leased bed or catching mullet in a cast net without a fishing license, it would be worth the gas it took getting here.

Wardens were trouble, even if you didn't hunt or fish. They could open a door without a warrant, stop you and turn you inside out without probable cause, and in the process if they found things they had not been looking for, that would be fine with just about any prosecutor in South Carolina. Sometimes the wardens chalked the boats that locals park all year at the county dock, instead of only three hours like the law allows. Then, like meter maids, they'd come back and write tickets for overtime docking.

Yancey did not want them to find him.

Jesus said a man shouldn't worry, that worrying was actively practicing unbelief. But Jesus had never been shot at, so Yancey reckoned He'd understand. Yancey worried when he gassed the tractor, worried when he checked the oil, worried when he backed up to the harrow and hitched it. But he did not worry once he sank the harrow into the ground and slipped the old Ford into double low.

There was more poetry here, the vibrato of the exhaust and the song of the creaking harrow, the tires tracking through the soft dirt, the sweet musk of earth mixed with pigweed as he turned it under. There was danger, too – the low limbs that could knock him off his seat, the soft edges of the ditches that could suck him in. He knew that over the years little Ford tractors had killed more men than most small wars. You must pay damn close attention on a tractor. You must not fall off and you must not flip over. Worrying is a distraction, so you must not do that either.

He finished with the first field and joggled up through the ditch and onto the road when the carburetor hung up again. The engine stuttered and smoked. Beating on the carburetor with the back of his big knife did not help. The engine lugged and labored and when it finally died, he knew it was over. He was walking home, about two hundred yards away, when he saw his shed door was open. That's when he wished he had thrown that damn motor in the river too. Yancey turned and headed in the other direction.

Gator Brown could not help him now. Neither could ol' Jake Simmons, gone to goofer dust, some of it sprinkled on a swatch of Susan

Drake's black panties. Saint John and Saint Jude, Saint Anthony and Saint Peter, Ogoun, Dambala and all the canons of the hoodoo saints everywhere in the world and beyond were struck dumb and helpless. He had no tractor and he had no boat. His shotgun was at the house. If they ran him with dogs they'd get him for sure. He jumped a ditch and scrambled through some bottomland hardwoods and thought about flying away like an old crow headed he knew not where. He crossed the old plantation ditch again and was, before he realized it, on a true course for Susan Drake's beach house.

He still loved her, great God he did, so strange and wonderful at her best. Wench, bitch, dirty *puta* at her worst. But mostly strange. It did not occur to him that had she not been that way she would have had no interest in him. Maybe way down deep inside, no matter how mad he was, no matter how hurt and jealous and crazy, he wanted to see that place one more time, the curling surf, the copper beach, the jasmine, still green but bloomless now way down deep into the fall.

But then he got to thinking. He could jimmie the door to get in, and stay away from the windows, keep the place dark at night. He could raid the freezer and drink her liquor and lay up each night in her big four-poster bed – *their bed*, as she had told him more than once. He could nose her pillow and maybe catch her scent. He had been safe there, safe in her arms and away from her husband, the dirty land-thieving bastard who never came looking for her and had an option on his daddy's land. Three days, maybe four, he would lie up in her house while he figured his next move.

But before he could get there he stumbled out of the brush into the front yard of the First African Baptist Church.

It was an old two-door country church – one door for men, one for women and children. They sat separately in a symbolic mortification of the flesh. They could not play footsie during the sermons but they could bounce songs back and forth like a volley ball.

The old building had a severe lean to the northeast from the great hurricane of 1893, but thick heart-pine clapboards held it together. There was a steeple and a bell with no rope. Nobody dared ring it lest it come crashing through the ceiling. The tin roof was wrinkled and rusty but kept out rain. The congregation had gathered every Sunday for the last 127 years, except the Sunday after they buried Dr. Martin Luther King Jr. over in Georgia.

Services were long and Baptist, lasting in various formats from nine o'clock in the morning until the middle of the afternoon. Come early and there was Sunday school. Come late and there was a sermon and a collection followed by fried chicken, collard greens, black-eyed peas, ham hocks and rice. The brethren and the sisteren drifted in and out, spending half their time hooked over the front porch railing. They smiled when they saw Yancey scurrying across the churchyard.

Well, boy, we been prayin' you up an' now you done come.

THIRTY

Squeezed-in between Brother Simmons and Brother Champion, Yancey was all itchy inside his head – like the moon was after him again, even though the moon was waning.

Brother Simmons was hatchet-faced ugly and blacksnake skinny, just like his uncle Jake. Brother Champion picked oysters in the old days before the Bloody Point Cannery on the south end of the island closed forever. Brother Champion was up in years but still had powerful oyster-picker arms and a neck like a longhorn bull. He wore a suit coat with a green metallic sheen that caught the light like feathers on a young drake mallard's head. The tag on his sleeve said Brooks Brothers but Yancey figured Brother Champion had cut it off another coat and stitched it on to prove his quality.

The Reverend Wiggins was holding forth from the ancient heart-pine pulpit and Sister Delisha was standing a few pews from the front and reading from the Book. Delisha was a pretty high-yaller gal, about the color of a Jumbo Honey Nut Cinnamon Swirl. Some folks said she was a *brass ankle*, but nobody could recall any Indians in her family. Her momma used to cook for the resort but her momma didn't cook any more because she was dead. Delisha still worked in the kitchen, though, and smelled of Wild Rose Hair Pomade and, very faintly, of dishwater.

Delisha stood on the women's side with some dollar-ninety-nine reading glasses balanced halfway down her skinny nose. *Maybe she did have some Yemassee blood in her from somewhere along the line,* Yancey thought. *She looked fine. How come the women who looked fine before I got sanctified still look so fine after I got sanctified?*

Delisha read from a dog-eared Bible so beat up around the edges you might think its previous owner had thrown it out the window of a pickup truck when the Book of Revelations started making sense. But nobody had thrown that book onto the road. It had been read hard and studied intensely and pondered over and passed down religiously for so long it was worn slap out.

"By the rivers of Babylon," Delisha read out loud as the congregants listened, "there we sat down, yea, and we wept when we remembered Zion ..."

The Reverend Wiggins was a strapping preacher, the hollering kind. He wore two-toned leather boots and a hundred-dollar Stetson hat. Called himself the Gospel Cowboy. He owned a little farm in swamp country south of Savannah where he raised Brahma bulls for the Coastal Empire rodeo circuit. He drove a Sunbeam Bread truck during the week, passing out Bible tracts all along his delivery route from Richmond Hill to Baxley that read, "Man Shall Not Live by Bread Alone."

He crossed over to South Carolina from Savannah every Sunday morning and always started his sermons with the same line: "God make de rough road smoode and de crooked road scraight and dat ribbuh ain' nuthin' but a footpath to de Lord!"

But this day he spoke of other waters, too. He held up his hand, cutting off Miss Delisha before she got very far along with her reading. "Wait-a-minute-now, wait-a-minute-now, Sistah, we gots to reason de Word a while!"

Delisha wiggled and blinked and remained standing while the Reverend Wiggins continued. "We ain' talkin' 'bout no Jordan Ribbuh, the one we all wants to cross someday ..."

"No!" another sister hollered from a pew just behind Delisha.

"Thank you, Sistah. We talkin' 'bout de Babylon Ribbuh dat nobody want to cross."

"Uh-uh," the sister moaned. "Dat right!"

The Reverend Wiggins dropped his voice down low and spread out his hands like Yancey imagined Jesus did when He calmed the storm.

"Yes, Lawd," the sister hollered again. "Amen, thank you Jeezus."

"Babylon hab book, he hab law and he hab ebery-ting. He hab great King Nebercaneezer, he hab de star watcher and de sci-en-tist and de doctor and ting. He eben hab de Hangin' Gaa'den."

"Oh, do Jesus!" somebody else shouted.

Yancey knew the Hanging Gardens was one of the Seven Wonders of the Ancient World but beyond that he didn't have a clue what they were – window boxes maybe, but somehow full-blown gardens?

But that didn't matter right then. The preacher was on a roll, his voice growing louder. "Babylomium come down like de wolf on de fole an' snatch up all de Chil'ren."

"Oh no!" several of the faithful cried.

"Oh yeah!" the Reverend Wiggins shouted. "Dey take 'em for slave."

At this, Brother Champion let out a big grunt from deep within his soul. There was a lot of breath in it, like the grunt a crapshooter makes as the dice stop rolling.

"Slave! Slave!" the Reverend Wiggins bellowed. "Dey take 'em off to duh mos' greatest nation dat eber be!" The preacher paused for an instant, gazed into the middle distance, then added, "Tenk God for a talkin' chu'ch!"

With that, every member of the congregation jumped up and commenced to stomping their feet and clapping their hands and praising Jesus and Abraham and Great God A'mighty and all His angels and all the other heavenly hosts. The boards in the ceiling and on the floor reverberated with hallelujahs and handclapping and foot stomping, all ricocheting off the walls, and the windows rattled in their frames.

It says somewhere in Psalms to make a joyful noise unto the Lord. Yancey's momma, raised up Episcopal, went to the baptizing of her yardman's ninth child. She came home and mopped her brow and mixed a Bloody Mary, sat down in her overstuffed easy chair in the living room and declared, "But not that joyful, for Christ's sake!"

Yancey got up last and sat down first throughout the Reverend Wiggins's sermon. Sometimes the Reverend's voice fell to no more than a whisper before slowly rising again to a cadenced shout:

"Babylon be sinful nation."

"Uh."

"Oh Lord, how dey sin."

"Uh."

"They be gamblin' an' cuttin'."

"Uh. Oh yeah!"

"They be shootin' an' stabbin'."

"Uh. Oh no!"

Then he got real loud again.

"De gal like de gal, and de man chase after de man. Dey dat marry done swap-off wife and lay round all drunk up and stupid half de time!"

All congregants were on the edge of their seats now. Some of them were smiling, some frowning, all nodding like they had each been there, or at least had seen the towers of mighty Babylon from a distance.

The preacher was now back to whispering again. "De Chil'ren ain' wanna do right." Then he whirled himself all the way around on one foot, raised up his arm, pointed a long black finger at Delisha and shouted, "What he say, what he say, what he say!"

It was like lightning had struck a big pine tree outside and turned the air blue. Everybody jumped and screamed and Delisha's reading glasses fell off her nose and bounced across the floor. When she bent down to pick them up, her dress stretched across her tight little rump and Yancey had second, then third thoughts about what he wasn't supposed to be thinking about after being sanctified.

Delisha got her glasses back on and stood up straight and resumed reading. "For they that carried us away captive, required of us a song, and they that had wasted us, mirth, saying, sing to us a song of Zion."

The Reverend Wiggins held his hand over his eyes and rocked back on the heels of his shiny two-toned cowboy boots. "I see 'em now, Brudahs and Sistahs, I can see 'em. You see 'em now?"

"We see 'um!" somebody yelled.

"Dem Babylomium march de Chil'ren clean-cross dat desert. Dey ain' hab no grits, they ain' hab no collard green. Dey ain' hab no fry chicken, no poke chop, no butter bean, no nuttin' like dat. Dey ain' eben hab a l'il dripple of water fuh to wet dey lip. Dey 'bout to drap over daid. An' de Chil'ren sat down fuh take dey rest ..." The Reverend Wiggins mopped his brow, which was dripping profusely even though it was way down in December. The acorns had fallen and the frost had nipped the fennel brown and the leaves left on the water trees and lying on the ground down in the swamps were red and yellow in the death of the season. Inside the church, there was no fire in the pot-bellied stove, but the air was hot and heavy with sweat and the sizzling work of the spirit. "But dey ain' get no rest. Dem Babylomium want 'em fuh sing and dance fuh 'um on de day of de Lord."

"Oh no! Oh no!" some congregants bemoaned in unison.

"Oh yeah!" the Reverend Wiggins said. "Now, what dat he say, Sistah?"

Delisha read: "He say, 'How can I sing the Lord's songs in a strange land?'"

The Reverend Wiggins raised his hands and a hush fell among them as heavy and as smothering as the sea fog on a wind-broke night. Yancey had trouble catching his breath, like he was winded and back in the woods and running from the law.

"Can we sing de Lord's song in a strange land?" the preacher asked.

"Uh-huh," somebody said, no more than a whisper.

"Can we sing, Sistahs?"

"Oh yeah!"

"Can we sing, Brudahs?"

"Hallelujah! Yes we can! Thank you, Jesus!"

"Well, come on y'all, let's sing!"

A couple of pews behind Delisha, a heavy-set sister with massive breasts rose up to her feet and belted out, "Wa-a-a-ade in the water ..."

And from the men's side came the response, "Wade in the water, Chil'ren."

And the congregation rose as one and sang the next line. "God gonna trouble da water."

"See dat man all dress in white."

"God gonna trouble de water."

"Mus' be leader of de Israelite."

"God gonna trouble de water."

"See dat man all dress in black."

"God gonna trouble de water."

"Dat be Pharaoh turnin' back."

"God gonna trouble de water."

And they worked their way through the whole spectrum – red, orange, yellow, green, blue, indigo and violet – finding a rhyme for each color, and above it all, the Reverend Wiggins roared. "An' Sweet Jesus say, 'Come unto Me all ye who travail and be hebby laden and I give you rest!'"

And one by one the members of the congregation stood and went up and gathered at the pulpit like a dark rolling cloud – some singing, some wailing, all with their hands above their heads swinging them back and forth with the music like marsh grass in the evening wind.

The Reverend Wiggins looked over the heads of the throng and saw Yancey still sitting, alone. He fixed him with a long index finger and a stare a lot like Gator Brown's from earlier, then called to him. "Mr. Yancey, Jesus say, 'You be shame of Me on earth, I be shame of you in Heaven!'"

Yancey leapt to his feet and rushed forward into the great mob of Gullahs, into their singing and their swaying and their praising of the Lord. He was happy for the first time in months, as happy as he had been slipping off to sleep in Susan Drake's arms.

"Oh we thank you Father God," the Reverend Wiggins hollered. "We thank you for de los' sheep who is found, for de one out of ninety-nine dat You went a lookin' for ..."

It was at that particular moment that a movement outside the window caught Yancey's eye: Two men walking along the brush line at the edge of the churchyard. White men – wearing dark blue pants and dark blue shirts and dark blue ball caps – all strapped up with cans of mace and guns and cuffs. And when they turned back toward the trees, Yancey saw the bright yellow letters on the backs of their shirts.

DEA.

THIRTY ONE

"What the heck's the matter with you?" she asked. She wore green hospital scrubs, and when she bent over to check his pulse, he could see down the V of her smock. She had cupcake-sized breasts in a push-up bra. He admired her tawny skin.

"Crazy, I reckon," Yancey said.

"You're not crazy," she said, "but you *are* in the medical wing of the Beaufort County Jail." She pumped up the bulb and the band tightened around his arm until his fingers went numb. She released the pressure slowly and, as he felt his pulse in his fingertips, she shook her head. "Too high."

"Let's slap your pretty little ass in jail and we'll see if yours goes up," Yancey responded.

She shook her head and her eyes sparkled when they met his. "I'll call the jailer, you keep talkin' like that. He'll cool you off."

"But you won't."

"No I won't. Just behave."

"Oh, I'll behave. What's your name?"

"Don't worry about that."

They'd caught him flatfooted and it was embarrassing. He felt like Claude Dallas, the Nevada wild man who shot two federal wardens for messing with his traps. They threw Claude Dallas into prison but he broke out and was on the run for a year and a half. When they finally did catch him again, it wasn't in some tepee way up in the hills like everybody expected. He was in the back bedroom of some girl's doublewide in Reno.

They caught Yancey in a bedroom, too, the upstairs one with all the mirrors and the four-poster bed. Shined a flashlight in his eyes and stuck a pistol in his face, and they rolled him over and cuffed him before he could so much as fart.

There were two of them in the bedroom, two more outside. They let him put on his pants and they let him take a leak, but one of the DEA agents stood at the bathroom door and watched while he did. They read him his Miranda rights while they waited.

They asked him if he had any weapons in his possession.

Yancey looked down at what he was holding in his right hand and said, "No sir."

"Any drugs?"

"I wish."

"Don't be a smart-ass."

"No sir."

"If you should remain incarcerated for an extended time, are there any minor children dependent upon your care?"

Yancey zipped up his pants and flushed the toilet. It was a tricky move with cuffs on. He wanted to tell them about Talladega, the pretty daughter he had been waiting for, but he did not. When they asked about pets or other animals, he wished he had taken time to get that Chesapeake bitch. There would have been some serious ass chewing when they tried to get in that door. But they would have shot her.

He asked what he was being charged with, and they wouldn't tell him. He asked for his shirt, and they wrapped one of their windbreak-

ers backward around his shoulders and zipped it up. The cuffs bound
his hands in front of him like a straightjacket.

The cops outside were talking to the security man, the one Henrietta
Ford trampled on her run back to Gator Brown's. "That's him," the
guard said. "Glad you got him. Don't need his kind on this island."

They hauled him across the water in their boat and they did not
give him a life jacket because they couldn't get him into one with the
cuffs on. Had they uncuffed him he would have jumped over the side
into the cold water. He'd have come up under the floating dock and
stuck his big nose between the floatation cells and hung there until
they decided he'd drowned and left. Then he'd get back to shore, find
some warm clothes and head to Savannah while they were dragging
for his body. He'd keep going south till he got where extradition was
just another gringo word. They must have figured this. He had run
once and he would run again and he would run forever. So they didn't
uncuff him.

Now he was in the Beaufort County Jail and didn't like it worth
a damn. They had taken his clothes and given him a baggy orange
jumpsuit. They had taken his shoes and given him slippers too floppy
to run in. They had given him an apple and a bologna-on-white-bread
sandwich for breakfast. They had given him nothing for lunch. There
was a cot on an iron frame with dried puke and God-knows-what-all
caked in the corners. There was a rough wool blanket and a stainless-
steel toilet with no seat and no lid that had been subject to a multitude
of misses. There was a window too small to crawl through. He looked
through it and saw pretty brown girls hanging on the chain link fence
trying to catch glimpses of their men inside.

Nobody came looking for him. About three in the afternoon, they
hauled him upstairs to the magistrate. He did not recognize her last

name but she looked like a girl he had gone to high school with. He sat down and leaned across the table and said, "Your honor ..."

And she barked, "Get your elbows off my desk."

He sat back in the chair. "Yes ma'am."

A bailiff sprayed the desktop with disinfectant, wiped it with a paper towel.

"Mr. Yarboro," the judge said, "you have been charged with assault upon a law officer, with fleeing arrest and breaking and entering."

"Yes ma'am. I was scared."

She held up the palm of her left hand. "This is no time for excuses. You are here to make a plea and for me to set bail." She paused. "I take it you're going to plead not guilty?"

"Yes ma'am."

"Do you wish to have your attorney present?"

Yancey figured it would take Mr. Wilton K. Ramsey, Esquire, a day or two to waddle over to the Courthouse, so he did not call him when he had the chance. "No ma'am. Just enter a not-guilty plea."

"You realize there may be more charges pending?"

"Yes ma'am, I figured that."

"And you also know the district attorney considers you a flight risk?"

"Yes ma'am. Figured that, too."

The magistrate leaned back in her chair and studied his face for a while. "But I find your ties to this community are such that you are not likely to run off. Am I correct in assuming this?"

"Yes ma'am. My people been here forever."

"I know you and I know your people," she said, taking off her glasses, shoving the papers aside. "Mr. Yarboro, I do not usually offer advice from the bench, but today I am doing so – off the record." She nodded at the court reporter, who nodded back. "Though you do not have a criminal record, there is a perception in this community that you have been in trouble before. You know what I'm talking about?"

Yancey thought of the dead burglars, the way the bullets has each left a purple ring around the holes when they went in. He did not want to think about what they looked like where the bullets went out. "Yes, ma'am," he said.

"You will most certainly be the subject of further investigation and I can tell you with reasonable assurance that it will be federal. If I turn you loose and you run, it is going to be very bad for me. Do I have your word you will not flee?"

"Yes ma'am," he said. "You got it."

She nodded at the reporter and they were back on record now. She took up the papers again, shuffled through them, picked up a pen and made notations. "Very well, I am going to release you on twenty thousand dollars bond."

"Your honor, I can't ..."

"That's already been arranged," she said as she peeled off the top two pages and pushed them across the table. "Sign this and I'll order your release."

Yancey scanned the first page: He would not engage in illegal activities, it read. He would not consume alcoholic beverages nor would he frequent places where alcoholic beverages are sold. He would not leave the state. He would show up for the next hearing at a time to be determined by the court. Any deviation from these conditions would lead to immediate forfeiture of twenty grand and reincarceration.

"Do you fully understand the conditions of your release?"

"Yes ma'am." But he was not thinking of those conditions at the moment. He was thinking of Susan Drake. Daufuskie Island Security had surely called her about him slipping the lock on her place, and now she'd sprung him. A man could not have a better woman than that.

They sent him back downstairs and locked him up again. After about the longest hour in his life, keys rattled in the door. "Come with me," the jailer said as he opened the cell. "I'll get Property to release your stuff."

They gave him back his clothes, shoes and wallet, and they made him sign for them. The guard behind the desk smirked and said he could keep the jumpsuit as a souvenir for twenty bucks, but Yancey declined. He was on the way out the door when he saw the nurse again. "Oh," she said, "I figured out why you were in the medical wing."

"Yeah?"

"Yeah," she grinned. "You are a prominent member of society ..."

She let the last words dangle like a rope, and she shifted on her feet the way Tara Lynn had in that strip joint before the trouble started. Yancey knew he could have that nurse if he took a little time. He could crawl into the corner booth of some riverside bar and suck a few beers and watch the tide and wait for her, the conditions of his release be damned. She would stop in on her way home and they would look each other in the eyes, then slide off to some no-tell motel out beyond the car lots and the pawn shops. Or maybe he'd just park her car in the oleanders by the docks and recline her seat and bend her over the back and pull down her loose green scrubs, and she'd leave footprints on the windshield while he drove it on home. There'd be great justice in that, he thought.

"Thank you, ma'am," he said, and headed for the door.

Sunlight never looked so good. Sea air never smelled better. *Hot damn, it will be good to see her,* he said under his breath.

But it was not Susan Drake waiting to take him home. It was

the Honorable Clarence H. Yarboro, retired and drunk. And it was Amanda Bethune Yarboro, just drunk.

His momma slouched behind the wheel of her battered station wagon with her ring hand hanging over the wheel. If it hadn't been for those dark glasses, her glare would have turned him to stone.

The engine roared, the tires gathered gravel and the car came at him fast. Yancey threw himself to the right, rolled over a curb and wedged up hard against a sizeable crepe myrtle. The car careened past and his daddy leaned out the back-seat window. His face was puffy and pale, like a biscuit too soon from the oven. He waved a fistful of papers and he shouted. "Bones? Bones?! Bones!!"

And the car squalled around the corner and they were gone.

 # THIRTY TWO

"I'da jumped if you'da jumped," she said.

He was on the island again. It was almost Christmas. The cassinas and the Savannah hollies were peppered with blood-red berries and the phone was acting up. Yancey figured it was tapped.

"I didn't," he said into the phone.

"I know," she said. "I didn't either. Would you'da jumped if I'da jumped?"

"Yes," he said. "We'd be like Running Bear and Little White Dove out there in Calibogue Sound."

"Didn't the raging river pull them down?"

"Yep. There's a mean current out there and lots of cold water. We would have lasted a total of twenty minutes."

"I'd like that," she said. "Together always."

"What?" he said, wanting to be sure he'd heard right.

A long pause. A lot of static.

"Look," she said, "it's Sherida's birthday and she wants to go to Savannah. You want to come?"

"Not particularly," he said. "Ain't lost nothin' in that town." That was not exactly the truth. But he never did find Tara Lynn again and Susan never found out about her. So it wasn't exactly a lie either.

Another long pause, more static.

"Look, I'm coming to Savannah next Saturday. You can meet me there if you like."

"Won't that be a little ... awkward?" he had asked her.

She laughed. "When did that ever matter to you?"

"Never," he said.

"I didn't think so. It won't matter. They'll all be there. Just say you came over for the evening."

"All who?"

"Oh, Sherrida and Casandra and the boys."

"What boys?"

"Jimmie and Johnny and Chip."

"Oh shit," he said.

"Don't worry, darlin'. We'll have drinks and supper and we'll slip off when nobody's lookin'. You'll be fine." She paused. "Won't you be fine?"

"Don't know."

"Well," she barked. "You coming or not?"

So that's how they wound up in the Savannah Westin Hotel, which was not actually in Savannah but just across the river on top of an old rice field after developers filled it with silt dredged from the ship channel and created five hundred acres of prime commercial real estate. An old tug made up to look like a turn-of-the-century riverboat shuttled guests downtown and back. Susan had a fifth-floor suite with a balcony and a view of the city lights. Giant freighters rumbled past them inbound, outbound. The *Asian Star* out of China, the *Nordic Trader*, with Panamanian registry, and the *Mystic Warrior*, homeport unknown. He sat, watched and drank good whisky.

She had gotten to the hotel first and was waiting when he walked through the door to her suite. He had not seen her in months and figured they would sit and face each other and maybe hold hands while he did some serious explaining about their fight, the break-in, the bust – everything. He'd have to kiss her ass, for sure.

And why not? He knew that the cops were not done with him, not by a damn sight. But he still had his land – at least for another year – and there would be another planting, another tomato harvest. He had been shot at and missed. Got thrown in jail and got out the next day. Christy and Mike were still on the lam. So long as they were running, he reckoned he wouldn't have to. His momma tried to run over him, but really didn't mean it. Now Susan Drake had called him and he was back on top again.

Sure, he would kiss her ass.

But he never got the chance. She was in this little skeeter-net black thing that didn't cover much and you could see clean through where it did. She had gained a few pounds, but great God, she looked real good! He got two steps inside the door and she was all over him, covering his mouth with hers, licking his lips with her tongue, tearing his shirt open and springing the zipper on his britches. And now his belly muscles were sore and everything was throbbing and he was watching ships go by and drinking good whisky.

The phone took off jangling – *kering-a-ring, kering-a-ring* – like hotel phones do, the red light flashing and all.

She jumped up and said, "Don't answer that!" She cut her eyes at him and placed her finger across her lips as she reached for the receiver. "Hello?"

Jimmie and Johnny and Chip and Sherida and Casandra were across the river at the downtown Hilton. If they all went outside they could wave to each other. The only thing Yancey felt like waving at them was his middle finger.

One of them – he could not tell which – was on a cell phone with Susan. "OK, darlin'," Susan said, smiling in Yancey's direction, "but let's not make it too early. Say about eight?"

The joint used to be the ground floor of a cotton warehouse before the locals figured it was easier to pick tourists' pockets than cotton. It had pretty good steaks and passable oysters, and Yancey had been there a couple of times some years ago. It was down along the riverfront and they had to enter from the street side and take an elevator down two stories to the bar and restaurant.

"Look," she said, "when we get off, you go to the bathroom and comb your hair and pee. I'll sit down, and you join us after a minute or two." They were standing in front of the elevator door and she had just pushed the down button.

"I don't need to take a piss," he said, "and I left my comb back in the room."

She put her hands on her hips. She wore a low-cut blouse and tall suede boots and tight black jeans that read "Lucky You" when she unzipped the fly. "You didn't bring a comb, you didn't even bring a toothbrush over here. You planning to spoil everything?"

"If I'm good enough to be your man at eight o'clock in the morning," he said, "I'm damn sure good enough to be your man at eight o'clock at night."

"You're a knot-head," she sighed. "OK, I invited you and I met you in the parking lot. You drove your truck?"

"No ma'am. Brought the boat."

"You're a little surly tonight," she said as they stepped into the elevator. "Maybe this will help." There was an ashtray in the corner, a big one full of sand. She reached into it and scooped up about a thimbleful, which she slipped into his left shoe. She reached over for some more and slid it into his right shoe. "Better now?" she asked.

Yancey hardly ever wore socks, and the grit felt good. But it wasn't beach sand.

Bong-bong, the elevator chimed. The silvery panels parted and they stepped out. The place was packed. As they walked inside, they heard the floor-man tell the doorman, "Don't let nobody else in till somebody leaves."

Yancey did not like crowds. He liked people, but in twos and threes. Every time he read about some nightclub fire where a herd of drunks crushed each other trying to get out the door all at once, he got the heebie jeebies. Susan Drake's friends sat on sofas around a low table across the room and looked over at them. Susan could not have surprised them more if she had led Yancey in buck-naked.

Nobody said a thing when they got to the table. Then Cassandra murmured, "My, my, aren't we brave?"

Chip called Susan "you little whore" as a term of endearment but Yancey did not see it that way. "I wouldn't talk that way to a lady, bubba."

"Good thing I didn't call her a slut," Chip slurred, raising his eyebrows and shrugging his shoulders. He pronounced it *thlut*.

Yancey had heaved his share of tomato crates, both full and empty. He had dug his share of post holes, pulled a ton of stumps and slung a cast net ever since he was a boy. He had a mighty right arm and a strong grip.

Quicker than you could holler *Balthazar*, Yancey yanked Chip up by his collar off the sofa, and across the carpet to pin him against a nearby wall. Chip's feet dangled. Everybody watched, gap-jawed.

Yancey had his thumb and index finger against the wall and Chip hung by his jawbones. Then Yancey slowly pulled out his skinning knife from his back pocket with his free hand and flicked it open with a turn of his wrist. Chip's eyes were as big as golf balls as they followed the point of the blade closer and closer to his nose.

It was like Mike and that shotgun. Yancey did not know it was unloaded and Chip did not know that Yancey would not carve up his face. Urine tricked down Chip's leg and splattered at Yancey's feet. Yancey turned him loose and Chip landed in the puddle, his back against the wall, his hand clutching at his throat and his lungs gasping for breath.

Yancey turned to Susan Drake. "Let's go."

"Wait just one minute, here!" she shouted.

Yancey scooped her up and threw her over his shoulder. Nobody tried to stop him as they left the lounge. There was a low beam about halfway across the floor.

"Watch your head," he said.

She quit wiggling and hung over his back like a sack of dead mullet.

"Step aside," the doorman yelled. "Let that man through!"

Yancey strode across the sidewalk with Susan over his shoulder and hailed a cab with his free hand. One stopped and Yancey opened the door, threw her into the back seat and dove in beside her. He flipped the driver a small wad of bills and said, "Find us some bad-ass blues!"

The cabbie dropped them off a few blocks west at a dive featuring bluesmen Dixon Day and the Rev. John Dogg, and they danced until the grit in Yancey's shoes felt good, until it was easy to pretend they had just met.

THIRTY THREE

I t was early in the morning way before sunrise as they strolled the
streets in a misty rain. Savannah is never so beautiful as in the rain
– cobblestones glistening and camellias laden with buds and gurgling
fountains glorified by the yellow light of old iron-and-glass street
lamps.

Yancey stopped and relieved himself on some azaleas. His zipper,
already sprung during the hotel roundup, was jammed. He untucked
his shirt to cover his fly and they resumed walking. From way down on
the river, the throaty blast of a ship's foghorn rolled over the rooftops
and through the alleyways.

"You shouldn't have done that," she said.

"Done what?"

"You shouldn't have done that to Chip," she said.

"He called you a whore."

"So did you."

"Did not."

"Yes you did," she said, "... in Spanish."

"Spanish is a loving tongue," he said.

"Not the way you speak it. You're a bully. You bullied me and you
bullied him." She was walking by herself now, having dropped back
ten feet or so, her arms folded tightly across her chest.

"I didn't slap you like you did me!" Yancey yelled without looking back.

"I didn't hit you *that* hard!" She spit out her words. "Didn't you tell me a man is supposed to get an ass-kicking every now and then?"

He stopped, turned toward her and said, "Only when he deserves it."

"You deserved it."

"So did your buddy back there."

Even in the half-light he could see those neon-blue eyes flash. "You, Yancey Yarboro, are a hopeless prick! You're crude and violent and insensitive!"

"Insensitive?" Yancey asked. He was about to bust out crying. He was going to say, *And you're some spoiled-ass married bitch from Atlanta, and I fell in love with you, damn me to hell.* He decided that if he went straight to hell for loving a woman like her, it'd be worth it. He wanted to say all this but the words hung up in his throat as they stood and stared at each other in the Savannah rain and he was about to cry but didn't.

Later, as they stepped aboard the water taxi for the trip back across the river to the hotel, Yancey fumbled for his wallet while Susan Drake pulled a twenty out of her purse, even though the fare was only two bucks each, and gave it to the mate. She leaned over and brushed her lips across Yancey's, poked her finger into the middle of his chest and pushed him backward until he stood on the dock by himself.

"You can't function like a normal human being when you're off that island," she said.

"Hell, I can't function on it," he said, "without you."

"Well, you'd better learn to. I'm cutting you loose."

"Why?"

"I got one asshole already. Don't need two."

The mate knew it was coming when he got the big tip. Six hours a shift, five nights a week ferrying drunks across the Savannah channel – he'd seen it all. "All aboard that's gettin' aboard," he said, staring Yancey down.

Yancey knew if he stepped back on board there'd be a problem and the cops would come quickly to solve it. There was the fight over Tara Lynn still floating out there, too, and God only knows what would happen if they found out he had just gotten out of jail in South Carolina for assaulting an officer of the law and stealing his M-16. So he just shrugged as the mate slipped the line off the cleat and turned and nodded to the skipper. The captain slammed forward the throttle and the boat lurched away from the dock. Susan Drake turned and walked into the cabin, standing with her back to the window.

There was something different this time in the way she moved, in the way she sashayed through the door. She hadn't rolled her hips like that before.

In half-light and a misty rain, Yancey could tell a buck from a doe, and if it was a doe, he could tell if it was in heat, had been bred or was suckling a fawn. He could not tell how he knew, only that he knew. He recalled Susan Drake's morning sickness and her odd cycles and the slight swelling of her belly and breasts, and he said to himself, *"Well, I'll be damned!"*

Yancey Yarboro understood most things natural. He knew the moon and its phases and the magic it worked in the sky and on the earth and in the sea. He knew the sound of the wind when it whistled off a wild duck's wing. He knew when big fish bit and when wild hogs rooted. He knew the smell of dirt, and when to sow and when to reap. He knew all this and more.

But just then, standing on a dock with his zipper jammed, Yancey figured he knew only two things for sure: That woman was carrying his child, and she would be back.

But maybe he was imagining all this. Maybe he'd have another talk with Gator Brown.